# The footsteps drew nearer...

Sweat beaded her brow as her fingers gripped the sheets. Inching to the edge of the bed, she rolled onto the floor and crawled away.

A hand grabbed her ankle.

As she flailed her arms, her hand touched fabric, a knit cap she ripped off. In the moonlight she saw his face.

"You saw me. Now I have to kill you." He yanked her hair and she screamed as pain shot through her. Who was this man? Diego had said something about switching cabins before she got here. Had this man come for Diego?

His hand clamped her throat, cutting off her air. As the room spun, she heard a thud and then the pressure released. She hit the floor, gasping. Strong arms lifted her and pushed her out the window. Diego.

Outside, he tugged her hand. "Run. Hurry."

Shaking, she struggled to speak. "What...is going on here?"

"I don't know."

But she knew. She'd stepped into a nightmare...and if her assailant had his way, she wouldn't live to wake up.

Ever since she found the Nancy Drew books with the pink covers in her country school library, **Sharon Dunn** has loved mystery and suspense. Most of her books take place in Montana where she lives with three nearly grown children and a spastic border collie. She lost her beloved husband of twenty-seven years to cancer in 2014. When she isn't writing, she loves to hike surrounded by God's beauty.

### Books by Sharon Dunn

### Love Inspired Suspense

*Dead Ringer*
*Night Prey*
*Her Guardian*
*Broken Trust*
*Zero Visibility*
*Guard Duty*
*Montana Standoff*
*Top Secret Identity*
*Wilderness Target*
*Cold Case Justice*
*Mistaken Target*

# MISTAKEN TARGET

## SHARON DUNN

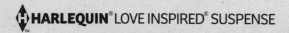

HARLEQUIN® LOVE INSPIRED® SUSPENSE

Recycling programs for this product may not exist in your area.

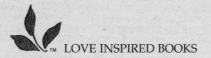

LOVE INSPIRED BOOKS

ISBN-13: 978-0-373-44728-2

Mistaken Target

Copyright © 2016 by Sharon Dunn

www.Harlequin.com

**Printed in U.S.A.**

I call heaven and earth to record this day against you, that
I have set before you life and death, blessing and cursing:
therefore choose life...
—*Deuteronomy* 30:19

As always, for Michael, friend and husband.
I miss you every day.

# ONE

Diego Cruz peeked through the open door of the resort dining and kitchen facilities.

The woman mopping the kitchen floor didn't look like a good prospect for conversation, but after days of isolation on the primitive island resort off the Washington coast, Diego hungered for any kind of human contact. He was an extrovert by nature. This much time alone was making him loco.

He stepped across the threshold. "Need some help?"

She jumped, placing a palm over her heart. "You scared me." She shot him a hard look before returning her attention to dragging the mop across the floor.

So she wasn't exactly *amistosa*. He didn't care. Even a hostile conversation would be better than pacing the floor of his cabin. Three days ago, he'd been a confidential informant for the FBI, working his way up the ranks through years of undercover work until he'd gained the confidence of the number two man dealing drugs in the Northwest. Someone had outed him, putting his life in danger. The Bureau responded by holing him up in no-man's-land until they could find the source of the leak.

Until the woman had disembarked from the ferry yesterday, the only people on the island had been Diego and a caretaker, an unfriendly old man named George who spent most of his time wandering into the forest with an easel and paints. George informed him the island was designed for people who wanted to detox from electronics. Diego suspected they didn't have the green to update, so being low-tech became the new marketing angle for the run-down getaway. To Diego, it meant no cell service and more boredom.

When Diego stepped toward the woman, her back stiffened. He smiled at her anyway. "So you're in my old cabin," he said.

She turned her back to him and slammed the mop in the bucket. "What do you mean?" Every word held a tiny punch, an effort to push him away.

"I started out in that cabin, but picked a different one. The view is better in the one I'm in now." The truth was the sight lines for the first cabin were bad. He was pretty sure the Bureau knew how to hide a man, but if he was found out, he wanted to see his assassin coming so he'd have time to grab his gun and defend himself.

She turned so he saw her profile. She was pretty, in an uptight, prep school sort of way, hair the color of dark honey, delicate bone structure. Despite the effort at dressing down in a flannel shirt and turtleneck, the clipped tone of her words and that perfect posture said she'd been raised uptown.

He'd grown up on the streets of Seattle and come up through the gangs. The gift that had kept him alive and now helped him with his work was his ability to read people. Seven years ago when a gang member's stray bullet had taken his *madre*'s life, he'd come back to the God his mother had prayed to every day. Becoming a

CI was his way of righting all the wrong he'd done as a teenager and maybe saving another homeboy's mother in the process, since he couldn't save his own.

"I like the cabin fine." Her gaze bounced briefly at him and then she stared out a dusty window. "I'm not here for the view. I'm here to do a job. In two days, the catering company I work for will arrive for a destination wedding. I'm getting paid extra to come early and set up and clean."

So she was from money, but she had to work minimum wage for a living. Now he was curious. What was her story? "Look, I'm going a little crazy here. Far as I can tell, you, me and that caretaker are the only ones on the island," he said.

"Spring is the off-season. I guess this place is really busy in the summer, so this was the only time the couple could get this wedding booking." She rearranged the cleaners and sponges in the supply-cart holder. "I'm sure they have a bigger staff then."

Her voice had a soft lilting quality that made his heart beat a little faster. "I was wondering if we couldn't eat a meal together or build a campfire. We'll see if we can get the old man to join us." George would probably not be interested, but he didn't intend for her to feel unsafe or wonder about his motives. He only wanted someone to talk to. He held out his hand. "So what do you say? My name's Diego Cruz."

She spoke slowly, taking a step back. "I'm…Samantha." She glanced down at his outstretched hand, but didn't take it. Feeling awkward, he let it fall to his side. "I'm really busy with work. I didn't come here to build campfires."

He couldn't understand her hostility. She didn't even

know him. He knew he should probably just take the hint and walk away, but he couldn't stand the thought of spending even more time with no one to talk to.

He stared out the window at the building next to the cafeteria. It was generously called the community room. It consisted of dusty furniture, tattered board games and stacks of *National Geographic*. The rest of the resort, and he was using the word *resort* loosely, consisted of five cabins and lots of trees. Samantha might not be a laugh a minute, but she was still the most interesting thing he'd seen on the whole island.

In two days when the ferry came back this way, maybe an agent would bring word what his next move was. Maybe the Bureau would tell him he could catch the ferry back to civilization. In the meantime, this kind of isolation and inactivity ate at his gut. He'd walked the island half a dozen times, memorized every fir tree and rock and explored the broken-down lighthouse at the edge of the island.

"You want to play a board game over in the community room?"

She lifted her chin and met his gaze with a look of cool disdain. Just more proof that she came from money—he'd got that exact look from more rich people than he could count.

"I'm really not interested in recreating with you," she said. "I came here to do a job."

Though she attempted to keep her words flat and emotionless, he'd picked up on the heavy intention of each syllable. She turned away from him, but not fast enough for him to miss the glazing of her eyes. She acted almost afraid of him.

"Look, I'm sorry. I just—" He stepped toward her.

She turned to face him. Her eyes grew wide with fear. She took a swift step back, accidentally brushing a full spray bottle off the counter. The cap must have been loose, because the cleaner spilled out across the concrete. She dived down to the floor.

"Let me help you with that." He grabbed a rag, knelt down beside her and started to sop up the liquid.

"I've got it. Thanks," she said.

"I don't mind."

His hand bumped against hers. She let out a small gasp, making eye contact for the briefest moment before jerking to her feet. She turned her back to him again. "Like I said, I don't want to visit. Please, just leave me alone."

"Suit yourself." He didn't want to upset her further, even though he saw now that the hostility was an act designed to push him away. Why?

She whirled around. Again, she gave him a look of hardened steel, narrowing her eyes. "I will." She brushed past him and raced out of the kitchen, leaving the door swinging on its hinges. Diego shrugged and decided not to chase after her.

He stood on the threshold of the kitchen. Moonlight allowed him to see her racing across the grounds to her cabin. Though he couldn't see her cabin through the trees, he heard her door slam. He stood for a long moment, shaking his head.

A mechanical and distinct noise filled the air. The hairs on the back of his neck stood up. The noise grew louder, and he was able to discern what it was. A motorboat. Someone was docking on the island. This island didn't get visitors.

Had someone come for him?

Fearing the worst, he sprinted out of the kitchen and ran toward the dock.

Samantha James's heart pounded wildly as she slipped into the safety of her cabin. The hammering in her chest wasn't just from the run across the resort grounds. That man, that Diego Cruz, hadn't made any attempt to harm her, but even the slight contact of his hand against hers was enough to awaken old fears.

She grabbed a pillow from the couch and tossed it across the room. She crossed her arms over her body and paced, waiting for her sense of peace to return. Nothing worked.

She slipped out of her clothes and jumped into the shower, allowing the warm water to soothe her. Since heated water was at a premium here, she kept her shower to only a few minutes. By the time she stepped out and had got into her pajamas, she'd calmed down...a little. She retreated to the kitchen to make some tea. She was doing all the things that normally helped her relax, but she still felt bent out of shape.

The nerve of that man being so friendly. Hadn't she made it clear that she didn't want to make friends? She came out here to do a job and for a little extra money. Since the crippling end of her marriage to Eric, she'd spent the past year keeping her head down. People didn't usually want to make an effort with someone as prickly as her...but Diego had. That kind of warmth and persistence was disarming. Her stomach twisted into a knot.

Then again, those qualities were the first things she'd been attracted to with Eric. She was shy by nature. She'd been drawn to Eric's ability to navigate social situations with such ease. Diego struck her as being outgoing, too.

She washed her teacup with brisk jerky motions. Through the window above the sink, she thought she saw movement. Her heartbeat quickened. Was Diego wandering around outside her cabin? That was kind of creepy if he was. She leaned over the sink to get a better look…but there was nothing there. It had just been a trick of the evening light. Still…something had disturbed the tree branches. Maybe the caretaker was out checking on things or it was a wild animal of some kind.

As she turned her attention back to the teapot, her fingers brushed over the knotted scars on her neck and her chest, reminders of why she'd been running away from herself for the past year, why she would never let a man into her life.

She had loved everything about Eric, his laughter and his smile. People gravitated toward him. He seemed to know what she wanted even before she said anything. She'd felt so safe when he held her, when she nestled her head against his neck, breathing in the musky scent of his skin.

But shortly after they were married, she saw a darker side to Eric. He'd taken out credit cards in her name and run up debt that drained her savings. She found out he'd lied about his education. His response to questioning his actions was rage. Fearing for her physical safety, she'd filed for a separation and begged Eric to get help for his destructive behavior.

He refused to admit that he had a problem—and had promised her that he would never let her go. She knew it wasn't because he loved her but because, as he put it, no one crossed Eric James. So when she refused to call off the divorce proceedings, he responded by destroying her life, as completely as he could. After he threatened her physically, she'd signed the house over to him.

To the other residents in Cambridge Heights, he remained charming Eric. Slowly, his subtle lies poisoned the rest of the tight-knit community against her. So thorough was his manipulation, they'd believed Eric over her. When her father passed away, she lost her last ally. Her mother had died when she was a little girl.

The final straw had been the car accident Eric caused by grabbing the wheel and driving them off the road so he could tell everyone that she had a drinking problem. The windshield had shattered, embedding glass in her neck and chest.

After the accident, she grew tired of the sideways glances and controlled whispers as she walked around Cambridge Heights. Eric's destruction of her reputation made it impossible for her to live in the neighborhood she'd grown up in. She had no one to turn to and no resources left to fall back on. When the divorce was final, she moved away, rented an apartment and got a job as a waitress while she tried to figure out how to put her life back together.

Seattle was a big city, and she was careful not to talk about her past to anyone. She used her maiden name on job and rent applications. Still, she didn't stay at any one job or apartment for very long. If she could ever manage to save enough money, she'd move out of the city.

She touched her neck again, taking in a quick, sharp breath. She didn't like other people to see the scars. They made her feel ugly, and telling the story of how she'd got them caused her to feel shame all over again. But in a way, she was glad for the scars. They served as a reminder that nothing was as it appeared to be and everyone had secrets. Especially men. For all his charm, Diego Cruz was probably a drug dealer or married or who knew what.

What was he doing staying here in the off-season, anyway? Even that seemed weird. He was definitely hiding something. She had been told that there would only be a caretaker on the island.

She shook her head. Why was she even letting him take up space in her brain? All she had to do was avoid that man until the ferry and the rest of the work party arrived. She did like her job with Evergreen Catering and the people she worked with. It was exciting to be part of a team making a celebration come together. Whether it was a wedding or birthday, bringing joy to others kept her from giving in to self-pity.

She crossed her arms and stared out the window at the darkness. Her encounter with Diego had her all stirred up to the point where she thought she'd seen someone outside. She didn't feel safe here anymore.

The metal of the lock on the door was cold against her fingers as she clicked the dead bolt shut. She retreated back into the cabin and pulled out the hide-a-bed in the couch. The cabin consisted of two rooms, a small bathroom and a second room that served as living room, kitchen and bedroom. She turned out the lights, slipped under the covers and squeezed her eyes tightly shut to keep the tears from coming. Anguish suctioned around her throat, and she wondered if there would ever come a time when she'd find a place where she could truly feel settled again. She'd been driven from her home. She didn't belong anywhere or to anyone.

The sound of her own breathing surrounded her in the

dark. She closed her eyes and waited for the heaviness of sleep to overtake her.

Instead, the muffled thud of someone breaking into her bathroom sent a shot of terror through her body.

# TWO

Diego stomped along the rocky shoreline, searching the inlet for the boat. He'd wasted precious time going first to the big dock where the ferry pulled in. He hadn't found any trace of the boat, but that didn't mean anything. A motorboat could pull in almost anywhere. Darkness shrouded the landscape, and he wished he'd had the presence of mind to grab a flashlight before he'd taken off running. He was sure he'd heard the sound of an approaching motorboat. Maybe it was just someone from a neighboring island out for a late-night boat ride, but he had to check it out.

He felt not only a need to protect himself but Samantha, too. She sure didn't need to get caught up in any trouble that might have come after him.

As he recalled their encounter, it was that moment of vulnerability he'd seen in her when their fingers touched that kept replaying in his mind. As if all of her hostility was an act designed for protection. She wasn't easy to figure out and that intrigued him.

Where was that boat? He jogged, scanning the shoreline. Why was he even thinking about Samantha? Hopefully, he'd be out of here in a couple of days, after which he'd probably never see her again. He wasn't sure what he'd be going back to. With his cover blown, he couldn't return to the hood he'd called home for the past seven years. He'd have to find some other way to make a difference.

He wondered if the Bureau had been able to sort out who had figured out his double life. He was deeply embedded in the Valley Hood Pirus and careful about how he communicated with the Bureau. He'd gone over and over his actions, trying to figure out what had led the dealer nicknamed Princeton, because he claimed he had an Ivy League education, to turn a gun on him and say, "I know who you are." Diego was lucky Princeton was such a bad shot—and a slow runner, especially compared to Diego's speed.

The days alone on this island had given him time to relive every conversation and encounter. Where had he slipped up?

Waves lapped against the shore as he made his way toward the water. Salt air filled his lungs. He continued to walk. Up ahead, he spotted the shadowy outline of an object. He sprinted along the beach, leaned over and felt the damp wood of the boat. He circled around the boat. He touched the motor at the back. It was still warm.

*This might have nothing to do with you.*

But if it did… Adrenaline shot through him even as he tried to remain calm.

They were five miles from the nearest island. He'd memorized the map in the community room as part of the futile attempt to get past his boredom. At that distance, it was unlikely that anyone was out for a late-night fishing expedition or a romantic rendezvous.

Maybe someone involved in the drug trade had seen

him boarding the ferry and was searching each of the stops on the ferry route.

He needed to find the owner of the boat. Best not take any chances. His gun was back at the cabin—he'd get that first and hope that no one was positioned to ambush him in the dark along the way.

He swung around and sprinted across the rocks and into the trees. His feet pounded the path that led to his cabin door. A peek through the window revealed no sign of movement inside. That didn't mean someone wasn't lying in wait for him. He eased the door open and slipped inside. With his back pressed against the wall, he absorbed the sounds, trying to detect anything out of place. He knew from his gang days that you didn't so much as hear or see an assailant as sense them. When a menacing presence was about to pounce, it was tangible.

His heart hammered in his ears, but he didn't feel the prickling of the hairs on the back of his neck that indicated danger was close. Waiting a moment longer, he took in a breath and eased toward the table by the couch where he'd left the gun. As part of his CI work, it was normal for him to carry a gun the way most of the gang members did. He was glad he had the gun now.

He reached out for the cold metal of his Glock 9 mm. Once it was firmly in his grasp, he walked his fingers across the table until they touched the base of the lamp. In a smooth unbroken movement, he clicked on the lamp, swept the room with his eyes and his raised gun. No one was there.

With the gun in his hand, he searched the bathroom as well and then the only closet. Unless the guy was small enough to hide in the cupboards under the sink, the place was clear. The tightness in his chest evaporated.

He slumped down into a chair, but before he could relax, a realization spread through him. He bolted to his feet. This wasn't the original cabin the Bureau had booked him into. What if the man in the boat had come for him, but thought he was in the other cabin? He raced out the door and up the dark path. Hoping, praying that he was wrong and that Samantha was safe.

Samantha froze as the footsteps drew nearer from the bathroom to the main room.

Another footstep padded lightly on the wooden floor. He was trying to be quiet and probably thought she was still sleeping. She closed her eyes, picturing the room. What could she use to defend herself? Sweat formed on her brow as her fingers gripped the covers. It was too late to hide.

Floorboards squeaked when he took another step. It was hard to gauge how close he was. Though she remained still, her heart threatened to explode in her chest. The room was almost pitch-black, but she knew the layout. She had to get away. Inching to the edge of the bed, she rolled out onto the floor and crawled toward the door as quietly as she could.

Not quietly enough.

Footsteps pounded. A hand grabbed her ankle.

She spun around, kicking wildly in the dark. She reached up toward where she thought his head was, grasping and scratching. Her hand touched fabric, some sort of knit cap. The man's heavy breathing was close to her ear. She clawed at the hat, ripping it off.

A break in the clouds sent moonlight streaming through the window and gave her a snapshot of his face. It wasn't Diego or the caretaker. How had this man got to the island?

He saw her in a quick moment, a look of surprise on his face. He wasn't expecting to see her. But then his expression was replaced by a look of determination.

"You weren't supposed to be here," he said. "But now that you've seen me, I'll have to kill you."

She flipped over on all fours and scrambled toward the door. He stumbled after her, crashing into a table and cursing. Something glass fell to the floor, shattering.

She reached out for the door but touched only air. Her assailant stomped across the floor, searching for her or the light switch. She couldn't tell.

A band of illumination appeared from across the room. She held her hand up toward her eyes, wincing at the blinding light of the man's flashlight. She saw him in silhouette as he dived toward her.

She screamed and ran toward the bathroom. Before she could close and lock the door, he slammed into it, knocking her down. A hand grabbed her hair and yanked her up.

"Too bad I dropped my gun. Otherwise this would be quick." His voice oozed with venom.

Pain shot through her scalp. "Please, I won't tell anyone." Why was he here? Diego had said something about switching cabins when he first arrived. Had this man come for Diego?

He released her hair, but the relief was momentary as his hand clamped on her throat and squeezed.

She fought for air and tried to angle away. He pressed tighter on her neck. She wheezed.

She felt light-headed, dizzy, as if the room were undulating. She was going to die here alone at the end of the earth. Who would even care that she was gone?

Any attempt to get away or kick only made her assailant's fingers grip tighter on her throat. She probably had seconds to live…and she did want to live, despite the sorry condition of her life. She twisted her torso in one final effort to escape, arms flailing trying to hit a target.

"No you don't, little missy." He yanked her closer, wrapping his free arm around her waist. His stagnant breath assaulted her.

Behind her, she heard a single footstep and then a thud before all the pressure on her neck released. She fell to the floor, gasping and coughing. Strong arms lifted her up and dragged her all the way into the bathroom. Diego locked the door just as her would-be assassin pounded on it.

Diego yanked her away from the door. "Through the window—hurry."

After slipping into the loafers she'd left in the bathroom, she jumped up on the toilet. The whole bathroom seemed to shake from her attacker slamming his body against the locked door over and over. Diego boosted her through the window, then followed her out.

Inside the cabin, the sound of the body banging against the door stopped. Light flooded through the cabin. Having given up on breaking the door down, the would-be killer must be looking for his gun in the cabin's main room.

Diego gripped her pajamas at the elbow, applying pressure. "Come on. We've gotta get away."

She was shaking so badly, it was a struggle to even form her question. "What…is going on here?"

"I don't know," he said.

Even without being able to see his face in the darkness, the tone of his voice told her he was lying. Deceptive. Diego knew why that man was here. What had she been pulled into?

He grabbed her hand. "Let's go."

Shots fired in the darkness. She may not trust Diego completely, but she couldn't stay here. They sprinted toward the trees. The gunfire made her feel as if her spine were being rattled from the inside. Diego didn't seem fazed by it. He led her deeper into the forest. Branches scraped her head and rocks caused her to stumble. He grabbed her before she fell. They ran for at least ten minutes.

Eventually, she stopped, out of breath. Diego quit running but he didn't stop moving. He glanced over his shoulder, rotated around to look at her and then began to pace back and forth.

"Who was that man?" she said between breaths.

"Some random crazy guy," he said.

She didn't believe him. He knew more than he was saying. Her throat went tight and she choked back tears. "I've never been shot at before."

He touched her arm. The warmth of his fingers sank through her thin pajama sleeve. "I'm so sorry you have to go through something like this."

He sounded genuine, but she couldn't see his face in the dark. And he'd lied to her already.

"We'd better keep moving," he said. "He wasn't that far behind us."

She wasn't so sure going with Diego was the best idea.

He turned to run and then glanced back at her.

Another gunshot tore through the air. Diego pulled her to the ground as a second shot boomed over them.

"He's close," he said. *"Vamos deprisa."*

He bolted to his feet and tugged on her sleeve. This time, she followed. At least Diego wasn't taking shots at her.

She held on to his hand, blindly hoping that he was

taking her to safety. Trusting a deceiver was never a good idea but what choice did she have?

She didn't know where he was leading her. She only hoped that she hadn't escaped one dangerous situation only to land in another.

# THREE

Diego's feet pounded the soft ground of the forest. Adrenaline charged through his body. He pushed his legs to move even faster. Samantha's grip on his hand was like iron as she kept pace with him. Minutes had passed without any more gunfire. Maybe they'd shaken the assassin.

It was his fault that Samantha had almost been killed. He suspected the man had come for him. If only he hadn't switched cabins.

Another thought hit him. The shooter had known which cabin he was supposed to be in. Only people in the Bureau would have access to that information. The leak might be within the Bureau.

He glanced over his shoulder. How close was the attacker? He couldn't hear anything. He was used to running for his life on city streets. Sound didn't carry in the forest like it did in an urban setting.

He brushed a branch out of the way before it hit Samantha, grateful for the time he'd spent walking the island. It made navigating in the dark that much easier—and it was an advantage their attacker didn't have.

Samantha planted her feet. "Where are we going?" Her voice was filled with suspicion.

"He came in a boat," he said. "I think if we can get to it, we can get away."

"Shouldn't we call for help? There must be a radio even if the cell phones don't work. The caretaker would know."

They were wasting precious time. "George is safer if we don't involve him." He'd already put one person in danger. He wasn't about to do it to another. And anyway, he wasn't sure they would survive while they waited for help to show up. Escape seemed like the best option.

She remained still, facing him in the dark. "Who are you?"

"I can't say." He understood why she was looking for answers. He hated the deception. She was an innocent in all this, but he had to protect his own identity. The less she knew, the safer she would be. "We really need to keep moving."

She responded to the urgency in his voice and took off running again. He sprinted to get in front of her and lead the way. They ran hard for another five minutes. Feet pounding, air filling his lungs.

She stopped to catch her breath.

She tilted her head toward the stars. Her words came out in fearful halting spurts. "He said…that because I saw him. He was going…to have…to kill me."

The images of the attack must have been raging through her head the whole time they were running. She wasn't like him, used to dealing with the trauma and violence. Moved by compassion, he reached up and placed a palm on her cheek. "It's gonna be okay. Let's get to the boat."

She jerked away from him. "It's going to be okay?" Her voice turned to ice again.

He spoke in a whisper while part of his attention remained tuned in to his surroundings. "It's not that far to the boat. We can get off the island."

"What about the caretaker? What if that guy is back there hurting him?"

She was thinking of others when her life was under threat. That said something about her character. He thought for a moment. "I think he'll be all right. He's after you because you can identify him. The old man is safe as long as he stays in his cabin."

He reached out a hand, but she didn't take it. He couldn't force her to come with him, and there was no time to waste convincing her further. He just had to hope that if he left, she'd follow. He turned and took off running. A few seconds later, her footsteps pounded behind him. He understood her hesitation in following him, why she was suspicious. But couldn't she see that he was trying to save her life?

They ran in an arc to the edge of the forest. The terrain changed from the lush debris-laden forest floor to rocky beach as the lapping of the waves pressed on his eardrums.

He glanced over his shoulder. Still no sign of their pursuer. He'd been on their heels and then nothing. What had delayed him? Had they really been able to throw him off or did he have some other surprise attack up his sleeve? "So you saw the guy? You could tell the police what he looked like?" Knowing who had come to kill him—who had got that confidential and protected information from the FBI—would go a long way to finding out who had blown his cover.

"Yes… I suppose. It was only for a quick second." Her voice sounded far away, as if she couldn't accept the reality of what she'd experienced. "I'm not sure how well

I could describe him, but if I saw him again, I'd recognize him."

"We'll get back to the mainland. I'll fix this," he said. He meant it. His lack of forethought had dragged her into this mess. That meant that it was his responsibility to keep her safe.

"Will you?" Disbelief colored her voice. She whirled around and trudged forward.

Her words were like a knife through his heart. He was a man of his word. Why would she doubt that? He shook off his frustration. Fine, he'd have to prove himself to her. He surveyed the dark shoreline. He knew from the landmarks along the beach where to find the boat. "Over here."

The boat was pulled halfway up the shore. He moved to the back of the boat to start the motor. The cold water of the bay suctioned around his feet.

"Once I get the motor started, I'll need your help pushing it out to deeper water."

She nodded and then turned back toward the tree line. She was smart enough to watch for their attacker without being told. For a girl from the burbs, she had solid survival instincts.

After twisting the throttle, he yanked the rip cord once. The motor sputtered but didn't ignite to life. He tried again, exerting more force. Still no results. He tried a third time. The engine sparked and then caught.

"He's here. I see him." Her voice reverberated with terror.

Diego glanced up, not seeing anything distinct. The shooter must still be close to the trees. "Let's go. We can make it. Jump in to steer. I'll push off."

As he pushed the boat off the sand, the first gunshot

came so close to his head his ear stung with pain. Samantha flattened herself in the boat with her hand still on the rudder. He jumped in. More shots were fired as the assassin made his way toward the water.

The motor clattered and then stopped altogether.

"We can restart it," Samantha said.

The shooter was too close. They weren't going to make it out of the inlet in time. "We've gotta bail."

He dived into the water and prayed that Samantha would do the same. He swam parallel to the beach, toward a rock formation that would shield them. He pulled himself up on the hard, rough stone.

A moment later, Samantha's head bobbed to the surface. He pulled her up. Both of them were shivering. He peered around the rocks. "He's trying to save the boat. Now's our chance to get away."

He slipped back into the icy water, swimming toward the beach but putting distance between himself and the man struggling to push the malfunctioning boat back to shore. The attacker would be as wet and cold as they were by the time he rescued that boat.

They hurried back toward the camp, running across the rocky shore and then into the trees.

A gunshot exploded behind them. Samantha stuttered in her step, releasing a scream that was almost a gasp. "Keep moving," he commanded. Gripping Samantha's hand, Diego sprinted into the shelter of the forest.

He zigzagged through the evergreens. The sound of the assailant close on their heels, footsteps and branches breaking, spurred him to run faster. Though they were shrouded in darkness, Diego managed to steer them back to the camp.

Several minutes passed without any additional gunfire. They slowed their pace, both of them out of breath and glancing over their shoulders.

"He can't be far behind." Diego resumed a jog.

Samantha ran beside him. "We have to get help. There must be some way to communicate with the mainland in case of emergencies. Let's see if there's a radio in the community room."

She was right—but it still wasn't a great option. It would take hours for help to arrive. Hours they'd have to spend dodging their attacker and trying to find a way to warn and protect the caretaker before morning came and he left the safety of his cabin. "That's where we go, then."

He turned and started running. She followed behind him.

Moonlight reflected off the metal roof of the community room. He surveyed the area around them. No sign of their assassin. Had they shaken him or did he have another trick up his sleeve?

They entered the community room. Samantha wandered around the small space opening doors and slamming them, searching for anything useful. She tossed a blanket in his direction after grabbing one for herself. "Where would a radio be?"

They were both shivering and wet. She drew the blanket tighter around her. Diego continued to search for the radio. "We should go back to the cabins and get dry clothes," she said.

He came up beside her. "He might be searching the cabins. That would explain why he didn't come here first."

He looked around. The room was maybe twelve by sixteen feet. There weren't that many places to put a radio.

He walked over to a small cupboard and opened it. Shook his head in disbelief. "No."

She turned toward him, voice filled with worry. "What is it?"

"The radio is here, but it's been disabled." That must be why the assassin was delayed in getting down to them at the bay. He must have seen them heading toward the boat but estimated he had time to destroy any chance of getting help before coming after them. The guy had to be a pro. Not some teenage gangbanger trying to earn his stripes. And how had he known to look in the community room? He must have had intel ahead of time.

Samantha couldn't conceal the fear in her voice. "What do we do now?" She lifted her gaze toward him, eyes filled with expectation.

He glanced out the dusty window, feeling the heaviness of what they were up against. "He's out there watching us. I feel it."

Feeling a chill, she pulled the blanket tighter around her neck. "We're sitting ducks in here."

"We're sitting ducks anywhere on this island. We have to get off it. I still say that's our best option." Diego paced the perimeter of the cabin, peering through each window. "There must be an emergency raft or something. Did you see anything like that?"

She shook her head. "The caretaker would know and maybe he has some way other than the radio that he uses to communicate with the mainland. Do you think we have time to get over to his cabin before the man with the gun finds us?"

"We might have to do that. George is going to come out of that cabin in a couple of hours and start wandering around anyway." Diego's expression made it clear he didn't like that option. He let the blanket fall to the floor.

His hand went to his waistband, brushing over a gun his sweater had covered.

She took a step back, wondering if the greater danger wasn't in the room with her. Her eyes fixated on the gun. "Just who are you?" She edged closer to the door.

He bent his head sideways and hesitated as though he were trying to come up with the right answer. "I'm with law enforcement. That's all you need to know." His voice sounded reassuring, almost gentle, but that didn't mean anything. His caring response might just be a manipulation.

How could she trust he was telling the truth? He'd lied about not knowing why the assassin was here. This was too much. She felt as though her already fragile world had been shaken to pieces. She wasn't in the habit of dodging bullets. Her legs weakened beneath her, and she collapsed into a chair.

He rushed over to her. "You all right?" He knelt on the floor so he could look her in the eye.

She thought she saw compassion in those dark brown eyes, but she didn't trust her own judgment anymore, not after Eric. "No…" Her voice faltered. "No, I'm not."

Dragging a chair across the floor, he sat opposite her. "Look, I'm sorry about all of this. I can't explain everything to you, and I know you think I'm lying. This is my fault. None of this would have happened if I hadn't switched cabins."

"What are you saying? That man came here to kill you?" Anger coursed through her veins. Lie upon lie. "So he's not just some random crazy who decided to make sport of hunting us down and killing us, like you said before." What if Diego was no better than the man out there? He didn't act like a cop.

"I'm asking you to trust me. I will get you out of here alive." He didn't break eye contact with her.

She didn't know what to think or believe. He seemed so sincere. She couldn't survive on her own. The man with the gun had made it clear he wanted her dead. Right now, staying with Diego was her only option. "How are we going to do that?"

Diego bolted to his feet and started pacing. "We need a way off the island. We need to keep George from becoming a target, too."

"We can't stay in here." She stepped toward the door.

He grabbed her arm and pulled her back. "You can't just run out there. Let's make sure the coast is clear first."

She yanked away from him, fighting off a rising frustration. "None of this would have happened if you had stayed in your assigned cabin. That man wouldn't have showed up and—"

He turned to face her, eyes like steel. "And killed me. While you slept. You would have been unharmed and unaware, but I would have been dead."

A rush of remorse filled her. "I didn't mean it that way. Of course I don't want you to have died so I could have a good night's sleep," she said. Her face warmed. She was ashamed for having said that. "I'd never wish anyone dead."

"I'm alive and you're alive and we're together. I can't help but see God's protection in all this." The intensity of his gaze made her take a step back. Eric had sat with her in church every Sunday. Her faith had been the final casualty of Eric's deceit. But she hadn't ever heard someone talk about God the way Diego did.

"God? I don't think He has anything to do with this." Her voice lacked commitment, compared to the passion she'd heard in his. She studied his face. Some unnamed emotion stirred in her gut. Whoever this man was, either his faith was real or he was a better deceiver than Eric.

Diego's expression changed as he whirled around, scanning the forest through the dusty windows. An instant later, gunshots shattered the glass. His body enveloped hers, taking her to the floor.

He rolled off her, the warmth of his protection fading. "Stay down," he said.

Another window shattered. The flying shards of glass were too clear a reminder of the car accident. Her vision narrowed. She couldn't move. Her brain fogged. She was shutting down, caught between painful memories and the terrifying present. She felt the strength of Diego's hands guiding her, almost carrying her as the bullets tore through furniture.

She found herself propped in a corner behind a couch. Diego crouched low and crawled toward one of the broken windows. He peered above the sill, took a shot and dived back down.

Several more shots tore through the tiny room. Samantha pressed hard against the wall. She couldn't stop shaking.

Diego took several more carefully aimed shots before he dived to the floor, resting his back against the wall.

Samantha's breath hitched. She counted to five as dust settled around her. The silence was almost as scary as the gunfire. It probably meant the shooter was finding a better angle of attack.

Her throat had gone dry. "Did…you get him?"

He lifted his head above the sill. "I'm not sure. Maybe he's just repositioning. Far as I know, he's only got a handgun. He can't be too far away if he wants to get a decent shot in."

Invisible weight pressed on her chest as she struggled to breathe.

He scrambled across the floor. "We should make a break for it." He hesitated in his step as he registered that he saw how badly she was shaking. "Hey, it's okay." He pressed her hands between his. "Most people don't handle gunfights well."

Her impulse was to pull away, but his touch and the kindness she heard in his voice had a calming effect on her. "All this is hard to deal with, but it is the…the sound of breaking glass that messes me up." She met his gaze. The swell of compassion she saw in his expression made her legs weak all over again. She wanted to believe that he was a good man.

His eyes searched hers. "You'll have to tell me sometime why that bothers you more than gunfire."

Another gunshot zinged through the broken window. Both of them crumpled to the floor. "He's getting closer. Let's get out of here." Diego reached up and turned the doorknob. "Use the building for cover. Stay close to me."

The night air chilled her skin as she pressed close to Diego's back. The soft fabric of his sweater brushed over her cheek. He pulled her into his side and put a protective arm across her torso while he surveyed the woods around them.

She peered over his shoulder, watching the forest. Her eye caught a flash of movement, the killer racing from the cover of one tree to another. "There," she said. He was dressed in black and had recovered the ski mask that hid his face.

Diego grabbed her hand and pulled her toward the

shelter of the trees. Again they fled. Though this time they had the benefit of early-morning light. After they'd run only a short distance, Diego headed away from the camp. Where was he going?

When he peered over her shoulder, his expression transitioned from pensive to fearful. He lunged toward her, pulled her to the ground. The impact on the hard rocks made her shudder with pain.

The bullet that hit a rock near her feet told her the plunge had been necessary. She looked up in the direction the shot had come from. The killer was there, barely hidden by the shadow of the trees.

"Let's go." He helped her to her feet.

"Aren't we going to warn George?" she asked.

"Too risky. We'll have to double back after we shake the shooter."

They ran along the beach away from their assailant. She was tired; she was hungry; she was wet and cold. She didn't know if she'd be alive when the ferry showed up or if they'd find a way off the island. Diego didn't seem to have much of a plan. More than anything, she wanted to believe that Diego was someone she could trust. At this point, she was staking her life on that hope.

# FOUR

Diego led Samantha toward the large boulders that populated the shoreline. He glanced over his shoulder. No sign of their pursuer. Not good. If he knew where the guy was, he'd feel safer. This assassin had shown he was tricky. Not seeing him meant he might be setting up an ambush.

Samantha slowed her steps. He let go of her hand and turned to look at her. She stopped completely.

"Where are we going?" Her voice conveyed a pleading quality, but her expression was lifeless.

He knew that blank stare. She was giving up. The trauma had been too much for her. His heart flooded with compassion toward her. No one should have to go through this.

"We can't go back to the camp. Not right away. He's probably expecting that, and it puts George at risk," he said.

She shook her head in disbelief. "But dry clothes. Food. The man who might be able to help us. All of that is back at the camp."

"There is a lighthouse on the other side of the island. There might be a boat or something there we can use." He still thought leaving the island was the safer choice.

He stepped toward her and squeezed her arm above the elbow. "If you want to stay alive, we have to outthink him. Do what he doesn't expect. I know this place better than he does—we need to use that to our advantage. By afternoon, we can sneak back into the camp if we can't find a way off the island."

His touch seemed to shake her from her trance. She met his gaze and nodded. "If that's what we have to do."

"Good, then." He turned and took off at a jog. A moment later, her footfall sounded behind him as she kept up the pace with him.

When they came to an open area, he stopped, still wondering what the assassin had up his sleeve. There were hills he could climb that would provide a view of much of the island. But if the shooter hadn't brought a rifle, he wouldn't be able to take them out at that kind of distance. This guy was clearly a pro. Diego knew he couldn't rule out that the killer had more firepower. He could have stowed a rifle somewhere when he got to the island.

Diego slowed his pace. The one assumption he could make was that the guy was behind them, not in front of them. "Why don't you get in front of me?" He could at least shield her from possible gunfire.

The lighthouse came into view. They ran toward it. He could smell the salt air and hear the waves crashing on the rocks. Diego yanked a dilapidated door out of the way and laid it to one side. He swept his hand out in a grand gesture. "Your castle awaits."

"My castle?" Her voice remained monotone but her face brightened just a little.

He felt a responsibility to pull her from the dark place she'd gone to emotionally. He was glad to see it had worked somewhat. They made their way to the top of the spiral staircase, entering a round room that provided a 360-degree panorama of the island. Though forest shielded some of his view, he saw no one approaching from any direction.

Samantha crossed her arms over her body. Her skin was pale, and she was shivering. The pajamas she was wearing were probably still wet.

He pulled his sweater over his head so he was down to a cotton T-shirt. "This is wool. It's almost dried out already. It pulls the moisture away from your body."

"But won't you get cold?"

"I'll be all right." Knowing that she might argue, he grabbed her hand and placed the sweater in it. The silky smoothness of her skin as he drew back reminded him of how fragile she seemed. She came from a much safer world than the violent one he'd grown up in.

Yet she'd revealed some core of inner strength. She'd pulled herself together enough to follow him to the lighthouse when she'd wanted to give up.

The cold, damp air soaked through the thin cotton of his T-shirt.

She lifted the wet pajama top at the hem. "I think it will warm me up more if I get out of this first." She glanced around as though looking for a private place to change.

"About halfway down the stairs, there's a room off to the side," he said.

She studied him for a moment, her gaze dropping to the gun now visible in his waistband. She turned and disappeared down the stairs. He listened to the sound of her footsteps fading. What had he seen in her eyes? Fear, maybe. She still didn't completely trust him. He couldn't really blame her.

He walked the circle of the lighthouse floor. He had a view of the ocean and most of the island. The cabins were hidden by the forest. Hopefully, if the assassin came for them, they'd have fair warning.

So far, he'd seen no sign of a boat or raft. They couldn't stay here forever, though. Or even for the thirty or so hours it would take for the ferry to show up. They needed food and water. Both of those things were back at the camp.

Samantha's footsteps sounded delicately on the metal stairs as he turned to face her. Her long dark blond hair framed her soft features. "Warmer?" he asked.

"A little, yes. Thank you," she said.

The color had returned to her cheeks, and her eyes appeared clearer. "You were smart to take the wet top off first."

"When I was a kid, my parents sent me to summer camp. They taught us city kids some wilderness survival basics at Camp Goodhope."

"Camp Goodhope? I went there, too." He'd been part of a program that sent underprivileged kids to the island where the camp was to teach them about community and faith. Though the message had not sunk in until his mother's death, the camp had been a haven from the violence of his neighborhood and where he'd first heard about Jesus.

She let out a breath. "That's kind of wild. I wonder if we were ever there at the same time."

"I would have remembered someone as pretty as you." The words tumbled out of his mouth before he could stop them.

Her lips formed a perfect O, but she didn't say anything. She took a step back, and he saw the fear emerge again in her expression.

He shook his head and dropped his gaze. Just when he'd built up a little connection with her, he had to go and mess up. What had made her so distrustful of him... of men? He only knew he needed to tread lightly around her. He wasn't lying, though. He did think she was pretty.

She cleared her throat. "I suppose we should see if we can find something to eat and some water."

"You're right that we need to search the place. Maybe we'll find a raft. First, though, we need to get dried out. We can build a fire outside down by the shore. The light-house will shield it from view." He turned toward her, putting on his best get-down-to-business face. "This is the high ground for now. He can't come for us without us knowing."

She turned in a half circle. "I hope he's looking for us and not bothering the caretaker."

*Bother* was kind of a mild word. "Yeah, me, too." The safety of the caretaker weighed heavily on him. Chances were if the assassin didn't want his identity known, he wouldn't seek the caretaker out to hurt him, but there was no way to know for sure. Diego headed toward the stairs. "Let's see what we can find." He brushed past her. Their arms touched briefly, and he felt a surge of electricity through his shoulder and into his stomach. They locked eyes for a moment before he headed down the stairs to find something—anything—that might help them survive.

As she rummaged through cupboards on the main floor, the sound of Diego's footsteps echoing through the lighthouse was unsettling. He clearly had the skills to keep both of them alive. She was starting to believe she could trust him in that arena, but what he said about her being pretty only opened old wounds. She'd caught the smolder in his eyes as she'd stepped past him on the stairs. That look only led to heartbreak and pain.

She searched several cupboards. Though run-down, the lighthouse wasn't overly dusty, implying that it had gone unused for only a short time. She found some brochures inviting corporations to bring employees to the island for outings, including a meal served by the lighthouse. Maybe the owner of the resort had let this part of the resort go due to a lack of funds.

She located a can pushed toward the back of a bottom cupboard.

"Find anything?" Diego's voice boomed behind her.

She startled, disconcerted that she hadn't heard his approaching footsteps. After glancing at it, she held the can up. "Pears."

"That's good. There's some liquid in them that will keep us hydrated." Diego had what was either a poncho or a Navajo rug flung around his shoulders.

She laughed. "That's a really good fashion statement for you."

He snorted, amused. "Hey, it's warm and dry."

She took a closer look. It was clearly a rug that he had torn a hole in to make it into a poncho.

"I'll look good for the fashion shoot later, don't you think?" he said. He struck a pose.

The levity of the moment lifted her spirits. Despite everything, he managed to see humor in something.

"I have a lighter. Let's build a fire out on the shore," he said.

She gathered together some paper and an old chair to build the fire and followed him outside. Diego broke up the chair and started the fire. Both of them stood close to it, soaking in the heat and drying out.

He reached for the can of pears. "Give me that. I can open it with my pocketknife."

She studied him as he focused his attention on opening the can. Diego's dark hair was still slicked back from having been so wet. His high cheekbones and strong jawline made him a good-looking man.

She turned her head slightly. The sweater she wore smelled like him, a combination of wood smoke and upturned earth. She sat down close to the fire.

Diego sat down beside her and tilted the can toward her. "Drink first."

Her stomach growled when the sweet aroma of the pears hit her nose. Embarrassed, she placed a hand over her belly as she drank down some of the liquid from the can.

Diego offered her his charming smile. "Me, too. It's been a while since I had any food."

She liked the way his comment defused her embarrassment. It showed a certain sensitivity she wasn't used to. He took a drink from the can and then handed it back to her.

She scooped up one of the pears with her plastic spoon. Her mouth watered when the fruit touched her lips. She handed the can back to him. By the time they finished the last pear, she felt a little stronger though still not full.

She noticed then that he was still shivering. "Why don't you try to get warmed up? Over by me away from the smoke," she said. "I'm not doing too bad. Thanks to your sweater."

He scooted toward her to get closer to the fire. She

jerked away when his shoulder touched hers. The response on her part had been almost involuntary.

Again, his steady smile conveyed that he was okay with her overreactions to his touch. She studied his profile. Under different circumstances, it would be so easy to relax around him.

After a few minutes, he jumped to his feet. "We can't stay out here long. We need to keep watch." He tilted his head toward the charcoal sky. "Looks like we might have some rain coming."

Just when they'd got dried out. They had no rain gear or even coats. The prospect of fighting hypothermia again—and the assassin at the same time—didn't sound like a good idea.

"Why don't you head up there and keep a lookout. I'll put the fire out." He jogged toward the shore, where he found a piece of wood to use as a shovel and scooped up some sand.

She made her way up the spiral staircase to where she had a panoramic view of the island. The rain began pouring out of the sky just as she heard Diego traipsing up the stairs. He was so tall he filled most of the doorway.

She stared out at the downpour. "I'm not going out in that. I guess we stay here for now." They were somewhat protected here at least. The thought of having to go back and be used for target practice made her chest tight. But staying in one place would make it easier for their attacker to find them. "Do you think it's just a matter of time before he comes for us?"

"I can't lie to you. He's looking for us. I'm sure of it," he said.

The thought made her shiver involuntarily.

He stepped a little closer to her, staring out at the forest and ocean. He was at least eight inches taller than she. His gaze fell back down to her neck.

The collar of her pajama top had covered the scars, but the sweater did not. She drew a protective hand up to her neck. "It was a car accident." That was all he needed to know.

He didn't answer right away, as though he were debating what to say. "I have scars, too." He lifted his shirt. He pointed to a mound of round white scar tissue. "Bullet when I was twenty." He turned to the side and stretched the collar of his T-shirt, pointing at the upper half of his pectoral muscle. "Knife wound when I was twelve."

She gasped as suspicions bubbled to the surface. "What kind of life have you lived?"

"I came up through the gangs in West Seattle. Turned my life back over to God after my mother died from a bullet that was meant for a gang member." The slight waver in his voice hinted at deep sorrow. "That's the life I've led."

She saw in his unwavering gaze that he was telling the truth. She turned away and stared out at the rolling waves for a long moment, absorbing the gravity of what he'd told her. "You've been through a lot," she said. His willingness to be so open almost made her want to share more about the car accident.

"I serve a man with deeper scars than my own," he said.

"Jesus, you mean." The name felt foreign on her tongue.

When she pivoted to face Diego, there was a weightiness to his gaze as he studied her, as though he could see straight through her and knew the condition of her own shredded faith. His eyes softened and she thought she saw compassion there.

"Why don't you get some sleep? I'll stand watch and then we can switch off," he said.

The mention of sleep made her whole body feel heavy. She slipped down to the floor.

He took off his makeshift poncho and tossed it toward her. "Use it for a pillow."

She folded the rough fabric and placed it on the floor. Even though the hard floor wasn't very comfortable, it took her only minutes to fall asleep.

She was awakened by Diego shaking her shoulder. "Your turn to take watch."

Her eyes fluttered open. She gazed out at the clear sky as she rose to her feet. The rain had stopped. "How long was I out?"

"It's late afternoon," Diego said. "Give me an hour's rest and we'll head back to the camp."

Her stomach growled. "Okay."

Diego's expression changed as if he sensed something. Slowly, he drew his eyes away from her and toward the window. His back stiffened. A high-pitched popping sound filled the tiny space where they were trapped. Plaster fell off the lighthouse wall. A bullet. They were being shot at.

# FIVE

"Get down." Diego's arm wrapped around her back and took her to the floor. The impact with the cold concrete sent reverberations through his body.

The dust the bullet had stirred up breaking the plaster settled and the heavy silence enveloped the room. They both lay flat on the floor facing each other, with their cheeks pressed against the concrete.

Her eyes searched his.

He needed to explain, to calm her fears. "I saw movement on the hill closest to us." So now he knew. The assassin had brought not just a handgun but something that could kill at a distance, as well. The odds were stacked against them.

"So what do we do?" Her voice trembled with fear.

He placed a calming hand on her back. "I guess we have to get out of here and back to the camp. If we can find a way to communicate with the caretaker without putting him in danger, we'll do it."

"George has probably left his cabin by now. He told me he spends his days wandering around the camp and out into the woods," she said.

Diego took in a breath as his mind filled with a sense

of resolve. They had been on the run playing defense since this ordeal began. Time to turn the tables. "We've got to set some kind of trap for the shooter so it buys us time to get to the camp and find George. This guy's hunting us. We'll hunt him."

Her eyes grew wide. "How?"

"I'm not sure yet." His mind cataloged through the terrain of the island. There must be some place for an ambush.

She lifted her head. "We can't go out the front. That's where the shot came from."

Her powers of observation under stress were pretty impressive. Diego glanced around the circular room. "We'll have to climb out one of the windows that faces the ocean." He crawled across the floor toward the window, careful not to rise up too high and be seen by the shooter.

She came up behind him on her knees. "That's a long way down and it's rocky."

He remembered seeing some rope in a storage closet one flight down. "Stay here and stay low."

To get down the stairs, he had to stand up and be exposed for a moment. He rose to his feet but crouched. As expected, another rifle shot zinged through the window and into a far wall.

Terror was etched in Samantha's expression. She crawled on all fours until her back was against the wall closest to where the shooter was. "Hurry," she said.

He scrambled down the stairs and found the rope. When he returned, Samantha still had her back pressed against the wall, her eyes closed and her knees drawn up to her chest.

He placed a supportive hand on her shoulder. "We can do this."

Aware that he risked being shot, he stood up and tied one end of the rope around the center pole. He crouched and dragged the rope across the floor and flung it out the window. It didn't quite reach the rocks below. They would have about a three-foot fall.

He turned to face her. "You go first."

She crawled across the floor and grabbed the rope. Heart pounding in his chest, he glanced over his shoulder. He moved so he would be between Samantha and the shooter when she was exposed.

She lifted her leg and crawled out the window. He watched her work her way down the rope. The roar of the ocean pressed on his ears. It bothered him that the shooter hadn't fired again when he stood up. That meant he might be on the move.

Diego held his breath as he watched Samantha come to the end of the rope. She hesitated, looking at the rocks below and then up at him. He nodded, letting her know she could make the drop. She let go of the rope, landing on her feet.

He took in a breath. Just as he grabbed the rope, he heard the thunder of footsteps up the stairs. His heart raged in his chest as he gripped the rope and climbed through the window.

The pounding of footsteps assaulted his ears. He peered down below at Samantha, who looked up, waiting for him. "Go toward the forest. I'll catch up with you."

She opened her mouth as if to protest, then clamped it shut and nodded. He had about ten feet left of rope and then the drop. The assassin, still wearing the black mask, appeared above him.

Diego rappelled off the lighthouse wall, causing the rope to swing. Hopefully, the movement would make him a harder target to hit. He watched as Samantha reached the edge of the forest and disappeared with a backward glance.

He tilted his head. The shooter lined up his shot. Diego let go of the rope and landed on the rocks below. The impact reverberated up his legs. A bullet hit the rocks a foot from him. Salt air filled his lungs.

He made a decision to run around to the front of the lighthouse and enter the forest at a different spot than where Samantha had gone. Why lead the shooter right to her? Adrenaline masked much of the pain from the fall. He entered the forest just as another gunshot stirred the earth in front of him.

Samantha stuttered in her step when she heard the gunshots. Her heart pounded against her rib cage. What if Diego was shot? She pictured him lying facedown, blood spreading out from his body staining the ground. She gasped for breath.

*Keep running. Stick with the plan.*

Another shot sounded. This one closer. She cringed and picked up her pace. She willed her feet to keep moving and walled off any thought of what might be happening to Diego. She had only a vague idea of where she should go. She remembered no landmarks from their run to the lighthouse. Her only clear memory was of holding on to Diego's hand.

She pushed through the trees, keeping one ear tuned to the sounds around her. She thought she detected footfalls. She stopped. Her heart skipped a beat when she realized it might be the shooter stalking through the forest, not Diego. Her feet pounded the earth. The trees thinned. Where was Diego?

She could hear the roar of the ocean again as she stepped out onto the rocky shoreline. Now she knew where she was. Out of breath, she slowed to a brisk walk. Her own footsteps seemed to grow louder as a sense of impending doom settled into her bones. Instinct told her to drop to the ground just as a bullet charged overhead.

Diego seemed to come out of nowhere, his hand suddenly warming her back. "He's right behind us. Head toward the cover of those boulders."

Crouching, she ran as fast as she could, diving for the big rocks. The shots stopped as they made their way through the maze of stones and then darted toward a line of brush.

The quiet settled in around them. Diego lifted his head slightly and looked around. "I wonder if there is a way we could trap him in these rocks."

After glancing around, she shook her head. "It's like a labyrinth in here. At best you could slow him down." Her words came out between panting breaths. She still hadn't recovered from their last sprint.

His face brightened. "I know what we can do, though."

She edged closer and spoke in a whisper, fearing that their pursuer might be in earshot by now. "What?"

"Fifty yards from here, there's a blind cliff. It doesn't look like it drops off. I'm going to lead him off in that direction. There's a ledge close to the top I can jump down on. You need to follow behind but not be seen, so you can pull me up from the ledge. He'll fall so far he won't be able to climb out. He'll have to go halfway around the island to get back to the camp."

The plan sounded incredibly risky. What if the assassin caught up with Diego or shot him? What if she wasn't able to get there in time? What if he missed the little ledge and fell all the way down himself? All the same, it was the best option they had. She took a deep breath and whispered, "I'll be right behind you."

He stood up. "I see him. He's looking for us."

They wove through more boulders until they came to the end of them. Diego signaled for her to stay behind as he burst out into the open. She watched as he slowed his pace, waiting for the assassin to make an appearance. The would-be killer slipped out of some brush and fell in behind Diego. He must have put his rifle down to run faster, or he had lost it somewhere.

Keeping both men in her sights over the hilly, rocky terrain, she ran toward the first clump of bushes, crouched for a moment and then sprinted again. If the killer looked over his shoulder, he'd see her.

The assassin had his pistol in one hand, but didn't take a shot. The sound of the ocean grew louder as she approached the cliff. Still running, she watched Diego disappear over the edge of the cliff and then the assassin was gone, too.

She willed her feet to move and prayed that she would get there fast enough and that the plan had worked.

She slowed as she approached the cliff, remembering that Diego had said the edge caught you by surprise. She peered over. The drop-off was maybe fifteen feet, but the cliff face was ninety degrees with no footholds or places to grasp. Strong winds off the ocean buffeted her.

The assassin lay on the rocks below about ten feet from the ocean. He twisted sideways and got up on his hands and feet. His gun had fallen some distance from him and was nestled in the rocks. She could see it from her vantage point, but she doubted he could.

She looked for Diego, spotting the ledge where he should have jumped, but he wasn't there. Instead, he was a few feet below there, clinging to the only tree that grew out of the cliff face.

He met her gaze and then craned his neck to the man below. "You'd better hurry."

Though wobbly, the shooter had risen to his feet and was scanning the rocks for his gun.

She searched the area around her as she fought off the rising panic that threatened to paralyze her. She found a sturdy tree branch and ran back to the cliff edge. "Grab this and use it to pull yourself to the ledge."

The shooter was closing in on his gun.

Diego's muscles flexed as he gripped the tree branch and inched toward the ledge. Samantha leaned back, using all her weight to hold the branch.

Diego reached out for the ledge and pulled himself up to it. She let go of the branch and peered over the edge. The shooter was kicking rocks around. It would be only a matter of seconds before he found the gun.

She thrust her arm down so Diego could grab it. Diego planted his feet against the cliff face. Even though there was nothing to hold him there, it lessened the pressure and pull on her arm. He used his arm strength to pull himself up and reach out for the cliff ledge.

Down below, the shooter had found the gun.

She held on to Diego's hand while he anchored his other hand on the cliff ledge and pulled himself up. A gunshot tore through the wind, grazing the base of Diego's shoe just as he pulled himself to the top of the cliff with her help.

By the time the second shot reverberated through the

air, they had managed to get to their feet and take off running.

They arrived back at the camp, both of them out of breath. They raced toward the caretaker's cabin.

Diego pounded on the door as his gaze darted around nervously.

Tension snaked around her torso. She glanced through the window. The sheer curtains allowed her to see that there was no movement inside.

Diego knocked again.

"It must be almost dinnertime by now. He's probably wandering through the woods with his easel." Or worse, the assassin had got to him before coming to the lighthouse.

As though he could read her mind, Diego said, "Unless he saw the shooter, the old man is still alive. Professional killers like this guy don't take anybody out unless they have to. They like things tidy that way."

It scared her that Diego knew that kind of thing. His world was so different from hers. She studied the trees, waiting for the assassin to burst through them even though she knew, logically, that he wasn't right on their heels. Not yet, anyway. "How long do you think it will be before he gets here?"

"To have to run in a big loop like that will take at least an extra fifteen minutes." He tried the doorknob. "Under the circumstances, I think it warrants us breaking in and seeing if there is a phone or means of communication in there." He pushed the door open. "You look around. I'll watch the windows."

She checked the living-room surfaces and opened some drawers. George's cabin wasn't any bigger than the guest cabins. She peered into a closet stuffed to the brim but saw nothing that looked like a radio or phone.

"If he has a phone that works out here, he must have taken it with him," she said, fighting off the seeping disappointment.

"We've got time. Let's go look for him around the camp and then out into the woods. We'd be okay shouting his name," Diego said.

"I think we should leave a note here, warning him to stay in the cabin and to get help."

Diego nodded. She found a pen and paper, and they left the note on the refrigerator.

They ran through the camp calling George's name without any results. They stopped outside the kitchen. "Let's hurry and get something to eat first before going to look for George in the forest," Diego suggested.

"I'm starving, too," Samantha agreed.

As they slipped into the kitchen, she caught Diego watching the forest. Both of them knew it was just a matter of minutes before the assassin made it back to the camp. She could only hope Diego had another plan, because she had no idea what they would do then.

# SIX

Diego felt a growing urgency as he opened and closed cupboard doors. "I thought there would be more food here."

"It's just left over from parties past. The cabins are stocked with food when they have guests. The wedding crew will be bringing all the food with them. Most of it is prepped ahead of time."

Hunger ate at his gut the more he searched.

Samantha found some bottled water and tossed him one. He chugged it, but soothing his thirst only intensified his awareness of the hole in his belly. She retrieved some packaged cookies and crackers.

"We're wasting time. Let's make a run for my cabin. I know there's food there."

She tore open one of the cookie packages. "Okay." She handed him a cookie.

He devoured it while he moved toward the kitchen door.

He pushed on the bar to open it, but it didn't budge. He pushed harder.

Feeling a tightening through his chest, he took a step back. "Let's try the other door." He worked his way back into the dining area already knowing that it, too, would be blocked, but he had to give it a shot.

When he got there, it was just as he'd feared. They were trapped.

Panic permeated Samantha's voice as she twisted the handle and then pulled. "What does he have planned now?"

"Step out of the way." He slammed his whole body against the heavy wood of the door, but it wouldn't give. The windows were too high up and small to hope to escape from.

"If he's not going to shoot us, what is he going to do?" Her voice trembled when she spoke.

Diego stared at the floor and shook his head. "I don't know."

Noises on the flat metal roof indicated that the shooter was walking around above them. Samantha edged a little closer to Diego. They listened to the slow careful steps. Thump. Thump. Thump. Like a funeral dirge. Their funeral. They followed the noise as it led into the dining area.

"He can't get in from up there," she said.

"And I doubt he has a gun powerful enough to shoot through the roof, even if he knew exactly where to aim." Diego's mind raced as he tried to figure out what the shooter had in mind.

Then he saw. "The fireplace." He wrapped his arms around Samantha and pulled her away from the fireplace. A whooshing noise sounded in the chimney, and smoke billowed out of the fireplace, filling the dining room. There was no fire, just some sort of toxic smoke bomb.

Diego dragged her toward the kitchen. He closed the door between the two rooms but smoke seeped under the door. He coughed as he made his way to the blockaded door. Even if they got out, the shooter was probably waiting for them, ready to pick them off.

The situation was impossible.

Diego had been in near-death experiences more than once in his life. He wasn't giving up so easily. As he dragged Samantha through thickening smoke, he knew there had to be a way out.

*God, help me.*

His foot hit something solid, a giant mixer on wheels. "A battering ram."

Samantha coughed. "What?"

"Help me smash this against the door."

His eyes watered from the smoke as they pushed the colossal mixer across the floor. "On three," he said and counted down.

Together they slammed the mixer hard against the door. It became more pliable after six times. Diego struggled for breath, growing weaker each second without clean air. "Again," he said. He summoned all his strength and pushed hard. The door burst open.

"Drop down." The smoke provided them with some momentary cover. The first gunshot caused a rush of wind by Diego's shoulder. He grappled to find Samantha's hand in the confusion. The smoke cleared.

He struggled to get a mental picture of where the shooter might be. The shot had come from higher up. He was probably still on the roof. That bought them time to find some cover while the assassin climbed down.

Samantha grabbed his hand. "This way."

At first he wasn't sure what she intended until a storage shed came into view. They dived behind it. Diego pressed his back against the rough wood of the shed and struggled to catch his breath. He didn't know how much more of this he could take. But they had to hold on until the ferry arrived, bringing help.

Diego's heart sank as he realized that the ferry would also provide a way for their attacker to get off the island. His deep sense of justice rose to the surface. He didn't want more hours of running only to have this guy slip into the shadows and escape when the boat arrived.

"We need to catch him," he said.

Samantha pressed her back against the storage shed, listening for the sound of approaching footsteps. Diego's words tied her stomach in knots. "What do you mean?"

"We need to catch him and turn him over to the authorities when that boat gets here," he whispered. He tugged on her arm. "First, though, we need to hide and come up with a plan."

Surveying the area all around, he rose to his feet and sprinted toward the trees. She cowered, expecting more shots to be fired. What was Diego thinking? They were not equipped to catch a criminal as determined and well armed as this one.

He led her up the steep terrain. When she was confident the assassin wasn't in earshot, she spoke up. "Where are we going?"

"There's an old zip-line platform up at the top of the hill. I need to get some sleep. We'll wait for the cover of darkness and then we'll set a trap for him."

"Why can't we just wait for the ferry to arrive? They must have some kind of security on those boats."

He stepped closer to her, locking her in his gaze. "I don't want to risk him getting away. Even if the ferry contacts the police right away, in the hours it takes them to get here, he could escape or he could kill us."

Her breath caught as she lowered her head. Panic caused the edges of her vision to fill with black dots. "I just don't know if I can do that."

"I'll come up with a plan that will work," he said.

It felt as if a cord was being wrapped around her chest. Hiding out and running seemed like the safer option.

He grabbed her arm above the elbow. "I know this is hard for you, but I will keep you alive and we will get off this island." He narrowed his eyes and locked her in his gaze. "Samantha?"

Her head cleared as she focused on the warmth of Diego's touch. His grip on her arm was firm yet gentle. She searched his dark brown eyes. "I wish I understood why this was happening."

His knuckles brushed over her cheek so lightly and so quickly she thought she might have imagined it. "Faith is believing in what you can't see. It's stepping forward when you don't have a complete picture. I'm asking you to have some faith in me."

Her throat went dry. Have faith in a man? It took her a moment to even process what he had said. Tears rimmed her eyes. "You have no idea what you are asking of me."

"I think I can guess." His voice filled with compassion and then he turned away from her.

She stared at his back. Something shifted inside her like a door cracking open and letting in a little light. If they survived this, then maybe someday she could tell Diego her whole ugly story.

They made their way up the hill through the trees.

Diego turned toward her. "How much longer until that ferry gets here?"

Her mind reeled. She'd completely lost track of time. "It comes tomorrow morning. The rest of the workers are coming on it to set up for the event, and then the wedding party will be on a private charter in the afternoon."

He tilted his head toward the sky, gauging where the sun was. "That's less than fourteen hours." He continued to walk and she trudged behind him. He got to the base of the tower. He stepped to one side so she could go up first.

She glanced back down the hill, but still didn't see any movement. She started up the ladder.

The platform for the zip line was made of thick plywood that had been warped by time and the weather. Diego handed her a package of crackers that he had had the presence of mind to stuff in his pocket. They ate in silence, both of them keeping an eye on the camp down below.

When he finished his food, Diego scooted up beside her. "I need to ask you to do something for me."

She turned to look at him, her face only inches from his. "What?"

"I haven't slept in almost twenty hours."

Her throat went tight. "You want me to keep watch." It was only fair. He'd done that for her at the lighthouse.

"At this point, I need rest or I won't be any good for either of us when we have to confront that guy again," he said.

She nodded, though fear made her want to refuse.

He grabbed her hand. "You see him coming this way, wake me." He squeezed her fingers and locked her in his gaze. "Got that?"

She said, "Yes," even though every muscle in her body tensed. She could do this. For Diego, for herself. She could keep them safe. Diego lay down on his side with his back to her.

She stared out at the early-evening sky. It took only minutes before Diego's breathing changed, indicating he was asleep. She scanned the camp below, not noticing any movement. Once she thought she saw someone in the trees by the cafeteria, but she couldn't be sure. The sky turned charcoal.

The sun sank lower on the horizon. Still no sign of the caretaker either. Had something happened to him or had he left the island? She sat up a little straighter. As darkness fell, she shifted to keep her legs from falling asleep. A light moved across the camp.

"Diego."

The light disappeared into her old cabin.

"What?" He sat up, fully alert.

"Either George or the assassin went into cabin four," she said.

"My guess is it's our would-be killer." He scooted up beside her and studied the camp below. "He must know we wouldn't go back there, so either he's going in there for food or for sleep. It's our chance to trap him. There are only two ways out, the bathroom window and the door."

Samantha crossed her arms over her chest. "I don't know why we can't just stay up here where it's safe."

"He'll find us before morning." He squeezed her shoulder. "I want this guy to go to jail. Let's give him a taste of his own medicine."

She steeled herself against the rising terror. Why did it feel as if they were going from the frying pan into the fire?

As they climbed down from the platform, Diego said a prayer of gratitude for the cover darkness provided. It meant they had to move much slower, but the degree of protection it gave them was worth it.

Samantha's hand slipped into his, probably not a gesture of affection. She just wanted to keep track of where he was.

They knew better than to talk. The assassin could be in the cabin or he might have slipped out. Diego's feet hit a patch of rocks that collided with each other. The noise made them both stop for a moment in their tracks. He gave Samantha's hand a squeeze to let her know everything was all right as they started walking again.

A light flashed to the side of them, on and off quickly. Adrenaline kicked into high gear. They'd been found. So much for ambushing him in the cabin. He must have left the cabin without using a flashlight.

They took off running down the hill. Diego let go of Samantha's hand, losing her in the darkness but trusting she would stay close.

A gunshot sliced through the silence. The shot was not even close to them. The gunman was having trouble tracking them in the dark.

Diego quickened his pace. He could hear Samantha right behind him. She let out a tiny scream. She'd fallen. He turned to help her up.

Weight like a brick wall slammed into him from the side. He wrestled with the assassin, but he'd been caught off guard, giving the other man the advantage. They rolled on the ground until the assassin had pinned him. Samantha jumped on the assassin's back, but he stood up and shook her off.

"Run," Diego said, jumping to his feet.

He hadn't meant for her to get into hand-to-hand combat. He'd handle this guy. He landed several blows to the man's face and stomach before the assassin slipped away into the trees. He must have realized he was going to lose the fight. Diego dived in the direction he thought the shooter had taken, but he couldn't see him. A moment later, he heard branches creaking in front of him. The shooter was headed down the hill where Samantha had gone.

Diego pumped his legs. He had a vague sense that he and the shooter were running parallel to each other as they descended the slope. Another shot was fired, this one close to his feet. He veered off in a different direction and slowed his pace to make less noise.

He saw a flash of light up ahead by the edge of the forest. Samantha must have run into the trees and now the shooter had found her. He worked his way toward where the light had been and entered the forest, careful to tread lightly.

The canopy of trees made everything pitch-black. His other senses took over as he extended his hand to feel what was in front of him. The lush scent of the evergreens and rich earth hit his nose.

Branches creaked, and he heard a noise that might be a footfall. How was he going to find Samantha in the dark labyrinth without alerting the assassin? He glided across the forest floor and pressed his back against a tree.

Slowly, he was able to discern the sound of footsteps placed far apart. Maybe it was Samantha, maybe not. He moved a little deeper into the trees. Then he detected the faintest sound of movement. He took a chance that it was her. She had to be close, not more than one or two trees away.

He extended his arm, feeling nothing. He pushed off the tree and took a step toward another. The scent of wool that had been wet hung in the air. He reached a hand out and touched the sweater he'd loaned her. He found her hand in the darkness and squeezed it.

He held her hand, leading her through the forest. A tree branch cracked when he stepped on it.

Three quick shots, all of them close, reverberated through the air.

He sprinted, away from where the shots had come from. The trees thinned and moonlight revealed the landscape.

They ran without stopping to a high bluff. The roar of the ocean was behind them as they both collapsed to the ground.

Samantha drew her knees up to her chest. "Do you think he followed us?"

"He knows the general direction we went. He might find us." He scanned the dark area below. He noticed she was shivering. "Are you cold?"

She scooted toward him. "A little."

He wrapped his arms around her, amazed at how comfortable she seemed with him being close.

"Do you still want to catch him?"

"I think we need to try. The closer we get to that ferry showing up, the more likely he'll just escape and come after us some other time," Diego said.

She took a long time to answer. "What should we do?"

"Let's move to the edge of the camp, watch and wait for an opportunity. He probably hasn't slept or eaten much either. He's got to be drained and weak."

They moved away from the bluff down the hill. All of the cabins were dark. The lights were still on in the kitchen. He was starting to think the caretaker had left the island. To get help or save himself, Diego didn't know.

They'd been all over the island, shots had been fired and smoke had come billowing out of the kitchen. George must have noticed *something*.

They came to the border of the camp that was more uphill and provided a view of most of the cabins.

Diego leaned close to her and whispered, "Let's sit back-to-back so we can see him coming if he locates us before we locate him."

She sat down in the grass. He felt the warmth of her back pressing against his. He watched the camp, looking for any signs of the would-be killer. He dozed off and jerked awake, half expecting to feel a gun pressed into his temple. The night wore on without either of them seeing anything. He wondered if maybe they should reposition but decided against it. The heaviness of fatigue overtook him. He went through cycles of sleeping for a few minutes and then startling awake, looking for an opportunity to capture the man who had tormented them for two days.

# SEVEN

In the early-morning light, Samantha could see the ferry through the trees. The tightness she felt in her chest subsided. "We made it."

She heard the distant chatter of the work crew disembarking. Diego had fallen asleep on the ground, his arms crossed over his body and his knees pulled up to his chest.

She shook him. "The boat is here. It's going to be okay."

He sat up slowly, pressing his palm against his forehead and then looking around. "He hasn't given up yet. You know that. I'm sure he'll look for another opportunity to get at us."

Her stomach tightened a little. "Then we need to get off this island as fast as we can. Let's get down to that boat."

"I need to talk to whatever security is on the boat. Have them search the island and watch to make sure he doesn't get on the ferry. I will contact the mainland once we're on board."

Diego rose to his feet. He swayed and Samantha pressed her hand under his elbow for support.

He wrapped his arm around Samantha's back, cupping her shoulder. "Let's go."

Considering what they had been through, she welcomed the support his touch gave her. Elise, one of the cooks for Evergreen Catering, looked in their direction as she came up the hill. Her bright expression darkened when she saw Samantha.

The older woman ran toward Samantha and gathered her in her arms. "What on earth happened to you, child?"

"Elise, I'm so sorry. I didn't get the work done and I'm in no condition to stay and help."

"Don't worry about it, baby. We'll take care of it. You look like you have been through the wringer. Is there anything I can do?"

"No. We just need to get on that ferry." Her voice faltered.

Elise glanced at Diego, who stood off to one side. "I won't ask and it's none of my business. You just do what you have to do, honey."

She touched Samantha's cheek, her eyes filled with compassion. Despite Samantha's aloofness, Elise had always been kind to her ever since she'd come to work for the catering company. When she saw the look of concern on Elise's face, the weight of all she had been through hit her full force and tears flowed down her cheeks.

"Oh, Elise." She wrapped her arms around the older woman, who patted her back and made comforting sounds.

"I'm sorry to have to do this, but we really need to get on that boat." Diego glanced around nervously, his gaze resting in the high spots. She knew there was a good chance the shooter was watching them even now, looking for an opportunity to take them out.

Samantha pulled free of the hug. "He's right." She swiped the tears off her face.

As they drew nearer the dock, a flurry of activity distracted her from the danger they still faced. Boxes heaping with decorations and flowers were being unloaded. Musicians carrying instruments made their way down the gangplank. She recognized many of her coworkers as they hauled plastic containers of food onto the island.

"Some party, huh?" said Diego.

"Five hundred guests." The happiness and excitement of the workers stood in sharp contrast to her own weary and anxious mood.

"You think they would have chosen a nicer spot."

"I don't know the bride or groom, but I get the impression this was a last-minute thing," she said. "The order for us to do the wedding just came in, like, two weeks ago. This place was probably close and inexpensive because it's the off-season."

The disembarking traffic was so heavy that they had to wait twenty minutes to get on the ferry.

Still tense, Samantha leaned close to Diego. Both of them watching and listening. It felt right to stand this close to him, their shoulders touching. Together they had gone through something that very few people would ever experience.

A break in the exiting traffic allowed them to finally board the boat. "When we get back to the mainland, I'll make arrangements for you to talk to…some people so you can identify our would-be killer."

"You're not going in with me." The longing she heard in her own voice surprised her.

"I can't. Too dangerous," he said.

His hand slipped free of her back, and she felt an emptiness she didn't understand. They'd known each other only two days. Maybe her attachment was just because of what they'd gone through. But what *had* they gone through? Why had all of this happened? She knew she would never get the whole story from him. He had said it was his fault, but she knew he wasn't a criminal. He'd proved that. He must be doing some kind of undercover work.

They found a table on deck. "I'm going to make some calls and see if we can get some sort of security from the boat to stay and search the island."

He left her then on the deck alone. His dark hair took on a blue shimmer in the sunlight. She watched him walk away and disappear inside. People milled around her. She closed her eyes and enjoyed the caress of the sea breeze on her skin. When she opened them, the buzz of activity on the shore caught her attention.

A realization jolted her to her feet. She scanned the dock and the high places behind it. She was too easy a target out here. She made her way into the interior of the ferry. She could see Diego talking to a man in a uniform through the glass. She caught his attention before sitting down. She studied the faces of the people around her. None of the people looked anything like the man who had tried to kill her, but that didn't mean he hadn't got on the boat and hidden away somewhere, out of sight. The ferry stopped at two more islands before it headed back to the mainland. Even if Diego had law enforcement meet them at the mainland, their attacker could still slip away before then, avoiding capture. Leaving him free to come after them again.

She rose to her feet and stared out at the vast ocean beyond the bay as fear rose to the surface once again. Maybe she could relax a little once they were in open water, but still, it was going to be a long boat ride.

\* \* \*

Diego found Samantha on the covered deck. He liked the way a faint smile graced her lips when he approached. He had to admit he wished there would be more opportunity to bask in the glow her smile created for him.

He held out a bag from the ferry gift shop. "All they had was touristy stuff, but I thought you could use some different shoes and pants." She pulled out the deck shoes and the sweats with the word *Seattle* written down the side of each leg.

He'd got a hoodie for himself. "If you want to get changed, then we can walk the boat and make sure that guy didn't get on."

"Wouldn't he hide?"

"Maybe, but he'd risk the crew stumbling over him. He'd blend in better if he pretended to be a regular passenger—but if he did, you might be able to spot him. We can have the captain confine him," he said.

After she changed, they walked all the decks. Samantha studied each male face as they passed.

Diego said, "When I talked to the ferry captain, he said he heard a report of an old guy picked up not too far from the island. George must have left the island, but the boat he used wasn't seaworthy."

"I assume he left to go get help once he couldn't find us and he saw the destruction in the community room." She shoved her hands in the pockets of her sweats.

"Probably." Their search ended outside the ferry café. She looked kind of cute in his baggy sweater and the sweats.

"I'm starving." She placed her palm on her stomach.

"Me, too." The café had only four tables and a counter

and a limited menu. They both ordered clam chowder and found a table that looked out on the ocean.

Salt-scented steam rose up from the soup as he crumbled crackers into the bowl.

Samantha dipped her cracker in the soup and took a bite. With each spoonful of soup, he felt himself relax a little. They ate without talking until the bowls were nearly empty.

He looked at her. "Are you still hungry?"

She nodded, wide round eyes focused on him. The look caused a surge of heat to shoot through him. He'd be sad to leave her on the steps of the FBI field office and never see her again.

"Let me see what else I can find for us to eat that wouldn't be too toxic." He pushed his chair back and moved to the counter, staring at the posted menu. The young woman behind the counter took a step forward.

"What do you recommend?"

"All our baked goods are made from scratch. Everything else is out of a can or box. The cinnamon rolls are the best."

"Cinnamon rolls it is," said Diego. "Two, please."

The girl swiped her forehead with the back of her hand. "You want those heated?"

"Sure." He glanced back over at Samantha. She ran her fingers through her hair and stared out at the ocean. He still wanted to know her better, to hear her whole story. Never in a million years would their worlds have collided like they did. He wondered if God had a hand in their meeting. He toyed with the idea that they could have something between them beyond keeping each other alive. With his undercover work, he'd always avoided relationships. It had seemed safer that way. Safer, yes—but lonelier, too. It had been a long time since he'd had someone he could rely on the way he'd relied on Samantha for the past few days.

The clerk pushed two paper plates heaping with over-size cinnamon rolls across the counter. Diego paid the clerk and returned to the table.

"Wow," she said when he placed the roll in front of her.

"From scratch."

She tore off a steamy piece and placed it in her mouth. The aroma of cinnamon surrounded him.

"These are good," she said. "My mom used to make the most wonderful cherry tarts from scratch. To this day, I associate that sweet flavor with memories of her."

He felt a stab to his heart. "Funny how that goes. I can't smell Poc Chuc marinade without thinking about my mother."

She locked him into her gaze. "That's something we both have in common. That emptiness of going through life without a mom."

"Yes, we both understand that." He relished the moment of heart-to-heart connection that passed between them.

She stared at the floor, and he shifted focus to consuming his cinnamon roll. The warm sweetness melted on his tongue.

"Thank you," she said without looking up.

"For…the cinnamon roll?"

"No, for keeping your word and getting me to a safe place." Tenderness glowed in her eyes as she raised her head and studied him.

Heat rose up in his cheeks. Even a little affection was probably a risky emotion for her to show. He was glad to see her take that chance. "I'm the one that put you in jeopardy in the first place."

They sat with the view of the clear sky, the scent of salt air mingling with the headiness of cinnamon and steamy sweetness.

She stared out at the dark rolling waves. "After what I've been through, it makes me think I'm strong enough to handle other things in my life."

Once again, she was being cryptic, and he questioned whether he should probe deeper or just let it go. He listened to the sound of the ocean, the steady rhythm of the waves beating against the boat. "Samantha? You can tell me anything." He reached over and put his hand on hers.

She looked at him, shaking her head. "You wouldn't understand."

"Try me," he said.

"I know you think I'm some sort of spoiled rich girl."

"No, I…" He couldn't tell a lie. When he'd first met her, that *had* been his assessment. His own insecurity about growing up a poor kid got in the way of seeing her for the complex woman she was. "You're more than that." His voice held unexpected passion.

Fear flashed through her eyes as she pushed her chair back, pulling her hand away from his. "You'll have to excuse me for a minute."

Diego watched her rush outside as a hollowed-out feeling invaded his chest. The café and the decks were almost completely deserted. People had probably retreated to the lower deck, where it was warmer.

His own insecurities had ended up hurting her just when she was opening up to him. He hadn't meant for that to happen. But maybe it was for the best. They'd be going their separate ways soon. He didn't know where she'd go from here, but he doubted there was a place for him in that life—even if he wanted there to be.

# EIGHT

Samantha leaned against the railing. The air chilled her skin a bit, but she liked the comforting sound of the ocean. The affection she heard in Diego's voice scared her half to death. It was easier when she thought all his charm meant he was just another Eric.

She didn't trust herself around him. If he only knew what a fool she'd been to fall for someone like Eric, he wouldn't like her at all. Maybe Diego would even be like her neighbors in Cambridge Heights and believe she was just making up stories about Eric to get attention. Besides, Diego seemed to have a chip on his shoulder about her having grown up in a wealthy neighborhood. She studied the dark waves of the ocean. It didn't matter how much money you had in the bank or how privileged your childhood was. Pain and loss came into everyone's life.

She heard footsteps. An older man brushed past her. There was hardly anyone out here. The sounds of laughter drifted up from the lower deck.

In a few more hours, none of her fretting over Diego would matter. She'd never see him again. She shivered, turning her head toward her shoulder. She caught the scent of Diego on his sweater. A gust of wind hit her. Time to go back inside.

She let go of the railing and started to turn. A hand clamped on her arm while another slid over her mouth and hot breath burned her ear.

"I said I would kill you and I meant it."

Her eyes moved from side to side. Except for the two of them, the deck was completely empty. When she struggled to get away, the assassin tightened his grip. His arm formed a V at the base of her neck and he pushed her backward toward the dark rushing water.

Her feet lifted off the ground. Her arms flailed as she tried to find something to hold on to. In an instant, she fell through space. Her body tore through the surface of the water. Waves rushed over her as she struggled for air. She shouted for help, but no one seemed to hear. The ferry grew smaller in the distance.

A chill settled into her bones as she spit out salt water. It was just a matter of minutes before hypothermia set in. She could see no rocks or landforms of any kind. A blinking light some distance away indicated a buoy in the water. She swam toward it as her muscles turned to solid ice. After only a few strokes, she could feel her body shutting down. Her heart slowed. She was coherent enough to know that she had only minutes before the cold killed her. Blackness closed in on her.

A familiar voice drew her back to the light. "There, she's over there."

Strong arms lifted her up out of the freezing water.

Diego held her, wrapping her in a blanket. "I saw you go over. I saw him push you."

She was lifted into some sort of rescue craft. But all she saw was Diego's face.

Oars stroked through the water.

"Go faster," Diego commanded. "This woman needs

medical attention." He turned again to look at her. "Hang in there for me. Can you do that?"

Her whole body had gone numb, but she thought she nodded. She opened her mouth to speak. No words came out. His hand on her cheek warmed her. She blacked out, and when she opened her eyes again, she felt herself being carried. There was blue sky and puffy clouds above her. Diego's grip on her hand steadied her despite the dizzy disorientation she felt.

As she faded out again, she heard Diego giving instructions to someone about her care. She shivered uncontrollably and her teeth chattered. Her last thought before she lost consciousness was that as long as Diego was there to boss everyone around, she was in good hands.

Diego paced while the nurse took Samantha's vitals. "Why isn't she waking up?"

"Mr. Cruz, she's fine. Her body experienced intense trauma, and it needs some time to recover. Her heart rate is already back to normal. Just give her a few minutes." The nurse left the tiny medical room on the boat where they'd brought Samantha.

He stared at her, her fine features and the porcelain skin. He'd only feel better when he could look into her blue eyes.

"Samantha?" he whispered, leaning close to her. She still didn't stir.

All of this was his doing. She'd run out on that balcony to get away from him. He had to make sure she was safe from now on. He wasn't going to leave until he knew for sure the assassin couldn't get to her. What that would involve, he wasn't sure. Maybe the Bureau could set up some sort of protective custody.

The boat security officer poked his head in the room. "We've searched the boat. There are no unaccounted-for passengers. No one matching the description you gave us, a tall man dressed in black."

It wasn't much of a description. Diego had only seen the man at a distance and never his face. "Thank you."

"Looks like one of the emergency boats was taken," said the security officer. "Could be he made an escape."

Diego nodded. Unlike the ferry, the attacker wouldn't be making any stops along the way, so he'd get to the mainland before they did. Maybe he'd set up an ambush. Diego would have to be prepared for anything. But at least they didn't have to worry about another attack while they were on the boat.

The security officer left and Diego turned his attention back to Samantha.

He smoothed the covers out around her then jerked to his feet and paced some more.

"Hey." Her voice was weak.

He whirled around. "There you are," he said.

Her eyes looked even bluer.

She lifted the covers and looked down at herself in confusion.

"They had to get you out of the wet clothes and into that hospital gown. The nurse took care of it. Are you warm enough? I can get you another blanket."

"I'm fine." She drew the covers up around her shoulders.

"You sure you're all right?" He wouldn't blame her if she was angry at him.

She twisted the covers in her hand. "How close are we to the mainland?"

"Twenty minutes," he said. "The nurse suggested you

get checked out at a hospital once we dock. I'll go with you."

"I'd appreciate that." She stared at the ceiling, biting her lip. "Diego, I'd feel better if you would stay with me when I talk to the people you need me to talk to."

"I decided to do that already," he said.

"Thank you." She shook her head. "I don't blame you for this. You're not the bad guy."

"But you thought I might be at one time," he said.

"Not anymore."

He detected a nuance of attraction in her words. Still, he needed to tread lightly, not scare her again. "Well, that's progress, then, isn't it?"

"Diego, there is something you need to know about me."

He leaned closer.

She studied him for a long moment before speaking again. "It's true that I had a privileged childhood." She bit her lower lip. "But I have nothing now. I was married and…" Her voice faltered and she looked off to one side. "…and the man I married was deceitful. He was a sociopath, he—" Her gaze came to rest on him once again.

What did he see there in her eyes? There was fear there, along with insecurity. It seemed as though she was waiting for him to dismiss what she had told him.

"I understand about sociopaths. In my line of work, I've met plenty of them. It takes a while to catch on to their game because they believe their own deception. But really it's all about what they can get for themselves."

Her whole body seemed to relax. "Yes, exactly. Thank you for believing me, Diego." She studied him for a long moment, a warm glow animating her face.

"Did you think I wouldn't believe you?"

"You'd be surprised how many people didn't," she said. She yawned and then her eyelids fluttered shut.

"Do you need to sleep some more?" He pulled up a chair and sat down beside her. "I'll stay right here and wake you when we dock if you want."

"Yeah, I'd like that. Just for a few minutes. I need time to change out of this gown."

She closed her eyes and turned her head as her breathing became deeper. He sat watching her sleep, glad that she trusted him enough for him to be a sentry.

The rest of the boat ride was uneventful. When the ferry pulled into port, Diego touched Samantha's shoulder lightly. "Time to go."

After she changed, he led her out into the bright afternoon. The activity on the wharf was substantial for the hour. She leaned close to him as he watched each passerby and glanced over his shoulder at the other passengers disembarking. The shooter would know where the ferry docked and might be waiting for them.

He hailed a taxi. "I'll call and have the people you need to talk to meet us with a car after we're done at the hospital. I'm sure it won't take long."

Samantha got into the taxi. He glanced around one more time. Coming back to the mainland painted a huge target on his back. Because the assassin had most likely made it to shore before them, he could enlist gang members to help run them down. He had no way of knowing how far down the ladder the information about him being a CI had traveled, but the more people who knew, the more people there would be with a grudge against him, out for blood.

He scooted in close to Samantha. Before, his proximity had made her stiffen. Now she seemed to welcome his being close. He craned his neck to look out the back window from time to time.

"Are they after us?" He caught the note of fear underneath her words.

He squeezed her arm above the elbow. "I'm just not taking any chances with you."

Diego took out his phone. "I have to get this charged. Can you memorize a phone number?"

"Sure," she said.

He recited it to her. She repeated it several times. "If we get separated, that's your lifeline."

The taxi rolled along for several blocks before hitting a red light. He studied the car to the side of them and then the one behind them. He recognized the driver as a gang member, the long hair and dark sunglasses. The grin on his face told Diego all he needed to know.

He whispered in Samantha's ear. "Get out as fast as you can. Blend with that crowd on the sidewalk. I'll be right behind you."

The light turned green and the taxi started to roll forward. Samantha pushed the door open. Diego dropped a twenty on the front passenger seat and pressed in behind her. The crowd enveloped them as the taxi and the pursuer rolled forward. Even if he'd spotted them getting out, the gang member would have to circle the block before he could get back around to them.

Diego pulled Samantha through the crowd into an expansive import store. "Are you okay with not going to the hospital? I think priority should be to get you to a safe place."

"Honestly, I feel fine," she said. "Physically, anyway."

They wandered through the store and up an escalator

to a floor where home goods and women's clothing were being sold. Samantha wrung her hands.

He looked around for someone with a phone and asked to borrow it.

If someone at the Bureau was involved in blowing his cover, he had to be careful about whom he called.

Someone who was totally disconnected from the secrets of the Bureau was probably his best bet. He dialed into administration. "Angie, this is Diego Cruz. Can you arrange to send a car over to the wharf by the alley outside The Import Place? I have a witness I need to bring in. It would be nice if you kept this between the two of us."

"I can do that," Angie said. "Should be about ten minutes."

All the time he'd spent chatting with Angie while he was waiting to make contact with an agent had paid off. She trusted him without question.

He clicked off the phone. "Ten minutes. Let's wander around. We're just a couple spending the afternoon shopping." He walked over to a display of china tea sets. "Here, look at this…honey." His voice sounded a little forced.

His theater act seemed to lighten the moment as her mouth turned up slightly, and she slipped in close to him.

"Yes, dear." Her voice sounded a bit wooden. "This set would look nice in our display cabinet."

Diego remained keenly aware of the crowd milling around them. Though staying out in the open was the best option, it left him feeling uncomfortably exposed. It would be nothing for a killer to put two bullets through their hearts and then fade into the crowd before their bodies hit the ground.

He ushered Samantha toward the shelves of cookware. He wanted to shield her from the level of worry he felt.

"This would be perfect for our dinner parties," he said in his best Thurston Howell III voice.

She snorted at his snobby accent. "Yes, we can put it right next to the gold-plated banana holders."

He leaned in close, changing his tone. "Let's head downstairs."

The fear returned to her eyes as he led her toward the escalator. They squeezed through the crowd and stepped out into the quiet alley.

"Hide behind that Dumpster." He pressed in close beside her and listened for the sound of an approaching car. If they'd been followed through the store, they were extremely vulnerable, but he hadn't noticed anyone.

His ears perked up at the sound of a motor. A car eased through the alley but didn't stop.

"How much longer?" She leaned close and whispered in his ear.

"Our pickup should be here by now." If this was nerve-racking for him, it was probably tearing her to pieces.

A car rolled to a stop. Diego poked his head up. He didn't recognize the driver, but the man had the FBI agent demeanor about him. Even through the distortion of the windshield, the clean-cut look and hypervigilant glancing around gave him away.

Diego opened the back door for Samantha. He was reaching for the passenger's-side door when a zinging noise pummeled his ear. The windshield shattered. The agent slumped forward on the steering wheel. Even though the doors were closed, Samantha's scream shot straight through to his marrow. He scanned the rooftops and up the alley but didn't see anyone. The shooter had to have followed them through the store. He raced around to the driver's side and yanked open the door.

Samantha had gone stone-cold silent and pale as a sheet in the backseat. The driver lifted his head and moaned. He was alive.

*"Muévete,"* said Diego, tapping the agent's shoulder. He wasn't sure where the agent had been hit until he saw the crimson stain spreading out from the agent's shoulder. He half lifted, half pushed the agent out of the way and got behind the wheel.

Samantha screamed. The gang member they'd seen earlier raced up the alley holding a gun. Diego shifted into Reverse and drove backward down the alley.

Samantha leaned forward in the seat, holding the semiconscious agent upright in the passenger seat. The agent's head flopped around and his eyes remained closed. Only his agonized moan told Diego he wasn't dead.

Diego cranked the wheel and turned out into the street. Wheels squealed and horns honked behind him. He hit the gas, zigzagging through traffic.

"Where are we going? Shouldn't we take him to the hospital?"

"Too risky. They'd predict we'd do that." The Bureau would see to it that the agent got medical care in a safe place. He shot toward an exit and took an on-ramp merging with the rushing traffic. When he checked his rearview mirror, he saw a white car behind them, but it kept a reasonable distance from them.

Five minutes later, he took another exit. The white car didn't follow him. He wove through city streets until he came to a parking garage.

"He's still breathing," said Samantha.

Her voice sounded calm, in control once more. He found a parking space and grabbed the agent's phone from his pocket. He dialed a memorized phone number and spoke the phrase that meant he was in big trouble. "No milk delivery today."

A voice came across the line. "Location?"

"Just below you," said Diego. "Section B."

"I'll be down in three minutes."

"We're going to need medical." Diego clicked the phone off.

Samantha's voice floated to his ear from the backseat. "They'd better hurry. His pulse is getting weaker."

# NINE

Samantha could still feel the thrumming of the injured man's pulse when the elevator doors to the parking garage burst open. Two men pushing a gurney rushed over to their car. While the injured agent was taken away, a third man addressed Diego.

"Come inside for debriefing." He turned toward Samantha. "Is this the witness?"

Samantha nodded.

"This way," said the tall man. He turned and started walking, their footsteps echoing on the concrete in the nearly empty parking garage.

The man led them up several flights of stairs into an area that could have been the waiting room in a doctor's office. A forty-something woman sat at a computer behind a high counter. The walls and carpet were a nondescript shade of tan. The only thing missing was a coffee table filled with outdated magazines people would only read out of desperation.

The tall man turned to face Samantha. "You'll have to wait here for just a moment. We need to talk to Mr. Cruz alone."

Numbness had settled into Samantha's bones. She nodded, not fully comprehending what was going on.

Diego offered her hand a squeeze. "I'll be right back. I need to make sure you talk to the right person."

She wondered what he meant by that. The men disappeared behind one of the four doors by the secretary's station. Samantha collapsed into one of two chairs on the far side of the room.

The administrative woman didn't look up from her computer or acknowledge Samantha in any way. When Samantha glanced down at her hands, they were trembling. Now that she was in a safe place, she was able to absorb the full force of what she'd just gone through.

Would the injured agent be okay? What would happen to her after she identified the assassin she'd seen on the island? Was she just supposed to go back out into the world after all this? How? She didn't even have her wallet or keys—her purse was still back on the island. She wondered, too, if she would ever see Diego again.

One of the doors behind the counter opened and two people, a man and a woman, stepped out and headed toward the outside door. Their conversation was about restaurant food, but Samantha saw the bulge on the man's side that indicated he was carrying a gun.

She laced her fingers together to stop the shaking. A man came through one of the doors. With his back turned toward Samantha, he leaned on the counter and joked with the secretary. Three more men passed through the room on their way out. They walked by the man who had his back to Samantha. When they left, the man turned so she saw his profile. Electricity jolted through Samantha's body.

The assassin. He worked here.

The assassin was with law enforcement.

The man turned back toward the secretary. Nothing

in his voice indicated that he had noticed her. She had to get out of there. If she ran past him to try to find Diego behind one of the doors, he'd see her for sure.

She got up as quietly as she could and scrambled toward the door that led to the stairwell. The door eased shut behind her as she raced down the stairs. She needed to find a way to alert Diego without the man knowing. Her phone was back on the island. She'd have to borrow a stranger's.

She heard the door open and footsteps above her as she turned onto the second flight of stairs.

Her heart pounded against her rib cage. She had to assume it was the assassin. She raced down the stairs and out into the parking garage. The door opened behind her, and she dived underneath a car.

Footsteps echoed on concrete, growing louder…closer. It was a small parking garage with only a few cars in it. Would he check under every car or assume she had escaped out onto the street?

The footsteps stopped. She held her breath and counted to five. The coldness of the concrete soaked through her skin.

A hand clamped around her leg. Unable to get away under the confining space of the car, she was dragged out.

She flipped over on her back. He let go of her ankle and gripped her shirt, yanking her up to his face. Her vision filled with his teeth and the acrid scent of his breath.

"I told you, you had to die."

*Not today.*

Her knee went up between his legs. He moaned in pain and let go of her. She scrambled to get away, crawling on all fours and then standing and running. She ran back toward the stairwell. He grabbed her from behind, pulling on her sweater.

The squeal of tires, a car entering the garage, caused him to let go. He didn't want to get caught in the act of killing her. He blocked her entry back to the stairwell, back to Diego. His voice fluttered with the nuance of challenge.

"Just try to get past me," he said.

She could hear the car moving through the garage looking for a space, but she couldn't see it. She turned and ran. Where was that car? The driver could help her. The footsteps of the assassin pounded in her eardrums. She didn't see a moving car or people headed toward the elevators.

She sprinted toward the exit. She squinted as daylight assaulted her eyes. There were no people on the sidewalk close to her. The killer raced out of the parking garage. She took off running.

Diego felt a sudden tightening in his chest when he stepped out into the lobby and Samantha wasn't there. The reception from the agent he'd talked to had been a little frosty, but they were willing to hear Samantha's story.

Agent Brown rushed in from outside. His face was flushed as though he'd been running.

"Decide to get a noontime workout, did you?" Diego knew Agent Brown in a cursory way from some undercover work the agent had been involved in when Diego had first signed on as a CI.

The agent shrugged. "Got to stay in shape."

Diego's cell phone rang and an unfamiliar number came up on the screen. He was glad he'd thought to charge it while he was talking to the agent. "Hello," he said.

Even before she uttered her first word, the tiny gasp

he heard on the other end of the line told him Samantha was in trouble.

"I borrowed someone's cell phone. I took a bus to Pioneer Square with change I had in my pocket. You have to come for me."

"Where are you in the Square?"

He heard muffled conversation as she spoke to the person next to her. Agent Brown lingered at the desk a few feet away.

She came back on the line. "I'm by the totem pole."

"I know where that is," he said.

Agent Brown made his way toward the exit, his gait casual and unhurried. Yet something in the way he left so suddenly after just being outside set alarm bells off for Diego.

"Why did you leave in the first place?"

"Diego, the man I saw on the island works in that office. I saw him. He recognized me and chased after me."

Diego's heart thumped a little faster as he stared at the door where Agent Brown had just exited. He'd had a feeling it was an inside job. "I'll be there as fast as I can. Stay out of view if you can." He was pretty sure Agent Brown was headed out to get Samantha as well, but he didn't want to make her more afraid by telling her that. "Hide and don't come out until you see me. Understand?"

Fear permeated her voice. "I'll try my best."

He grabbed a key from Angie for one of the agency's cars and raced down the stairs to the parking garage. His heart was pounding by the time he jumped into the car and turned the key in the ignition.

Agent Brown had only a five-minute head start on him. He knew Samantha was in the Square but he didn't know she was by the totem pole. Diego knew all the shortcuts through the city and how to avoid the streets with the heavy traffic. He pushed the accelerator to the floor and sped down a side street. He cleared his mind of the images that threatened to shut him down. Pictures of Samantha dying would make it impossible to focus. He needed to get to her first. That was the mission.

He saw traffic jammed up ahead, around the bus tunnel exit. He pulled over and ran the remaining three blocks, quickly arriving at the totem pole. Samantha wasn't there. Where was she hiding? Maybe in a shop.

Heart pounding, he scanned the faces in the crowd, seeing no sign of Agent Brown. Maybe he wasn't even a part of this. He could have been just leaving to get coffee. He hadn't had time to ask Samantha to describe the agent.

He milled through the crowd, not spotting Agent Brown or Samantha. He entertained the thought that he was too late for only a second. She was here and he would find her.

He checked the window front of a café and then stepped into a pet store. The store clerk, who had a white bird on his shoulder, looked at him. "Did a pretty woman in a wool sweater with light brown hair come in here?" Diego asked.

The clerk shook his head and Diego felt as if he'd been punched in the stomach. She had to be okay. He just needed to make himself visible, and she'd come to him. He walked past a street musician playing a guitar then paced a wide circle around the totem pole before sitting on a bench. His eyes traveled upward. She was standing at a second-story window. She offered him a tiny wave.

His heart surged. He ran across the Square and into the building. Samantha met him on the stairs.

"The agent who tried to kill us is down in the Square," she said. "I could see him from where I was hiding."

"Where is he?"

"Across the Square headed away from the totem pole," she said.

Searching for a back exit in the building would take too much time. "Let's just slip out and blend with the crowd. I'm parked three blocks away. We can make it."

He put his arm around her. "Just be casual. Don't call attention."

"We're just a couple out for a stroll." Tension threaded through her voice.

He didn't see Agent Brown among any of the crowds. Most of these people were meandering and peering in shop windows. Agent Brown would be striding with a purpose. Even that kind of movement would make him stand out.

Samantha's gaze darted around, as well. She gasped. "He's there by the bookshop."

Agent Brown's back was turned toward them. They needed to hide. Diego saw the entrance for the Underground Seattle tour and pulled her toward it just as Agent Brown turned.

She pressed close to him. "Do you think he saw us?"

Diego shook his head. "Let's find a different way out."

Seattle was a city built on top of a city. Repeated floods from tides had made builders raise the city's elevation. They moved past what used to be the shops and sidewalks of Seattle.

Footsteps echoed behind them, but they didn't sound hurried.

"They run tours through here," she said.

They couldn't take any chances that Agent Brown

might be one of the people behind them. Diego rushed them past a brick wall that had historical photos on it. They could hear footsteps behind them but no voices. Only one person. Metal pipes, shop and hotel signs and debris cluttered the area by the brick walls. The sounds of the city above them filtered down when they stepped beneath a grate where light shone through.

They came to a newer structure, a gift shop. Diego yanked open the door just as Agent Brown came around the corner.

The store clerk straightened some T-shirts. A look of surprise crossed her expression. "The group isn't supposed to come through for another hour."

"The way out?" said Diego.

The clerk pointed at a door on the other side of the shop. They raced toward it, up the stairs and out into the sunlight.

"This way. I'm parked just up the street." Diego took off running and Samantha sprinted beside him.

Feeling the weight of a gaze on him, he craned his neck.

Agent Brown was about ten yards from them. Diego pointed to their ride. "Get in the car."

She yanked open the passenger's-side door while he got behind the wheel. Agent Brown wouldn't risk shooting them here, not with all the people around. He pulled away from the curb just as Agent Brown reached them. He took the butt of his gun and slammed it into the windshield. Samantha jerked her head back, but she didn't scream. When he glanced over at her, all the color had drained from her face.

Diego got the car up to speed and pulled out into traffic. In his rearview mirror, he saw Agent Brown running in the opposite direction, probably to get to his car.

As he wove through the busy city streets, Diego's thoughts raced. Why had Agent Brown turned? Probably money. It was always money.

"Where are we going?"

"We need to let the Bureau know that Agent Brown is dirty, and they will bring us in." He handed her his phone as he turned up a quiet residential street. "Press speed dial 2 and explain what has happened. Tell them we will meet them at Discovery Park. I don't want to risk going back to the Bureau office and having Agent Brown be waiting there for us."

She looked at the phone. "Who will I be talking to?"

"Agent Lister is second in command for the Seattle office. I've never met him. I'm only supposed to call that number in extreme emergencies."

Samantha dialed the number and explained their situation. She hung up. "Two agents will meet us there in ten minutes."

He drove to Discovery Park. They got out of the car. Samantha sat on the hood while Diego paced. Fifty yards away, children played with kites, their laughter floating through the air. The park was a series of trails and woods that looked out on Puget Sound. He could hear the ocean in the distance. He tried to let the peaceful surroundings soothe his anxiety. Hopefully, this whole mess would be taken care of soon.

They both wandered through the lot and onto a nearby trail. She crossed her arms and stared at the children playing.

He liked the way Samantha smiled when she looked at the children. "Do you ever think about having kids?"

He asked the question to get her mind off what had just happened.

"Once upon a time, I thought that was going to be my life." A tone of sadness sneaked into her words. "But not anymore." She squared her shoulders and lifted her chin. "How about you?"

"I've got nieces and nephews. I kind of think my purpose in life is to work to protect them and all the other kids trying to grow up in the hood."

"So you don't have any little Diegos running around anywhere?"

"I wasn't a saint before I gave my life over to God, but no. No sons or daughters that I know of."

"Both of our lives got derailed from what would be a normal path," she said.

He met her gaze and nodded. "That much is true. We have that in common."

"When you say that…it seems like you are thinking about what we *don't* have in common."

"We are just from different worlds, Samantha. Very different worlds."

Her expression changed as though a shadow had descended across her face. He wondered why she had asked the question in the first place. Was she picturing the two of them together raising a family or was she just making conversation, trying to get to know him better? It didn't matter. As hard as she tried to find things they had in common, he knew their differences were too great.

His mission and his life were not in the burbs raising children, driving a minivan and being middle class. That was the life she should have—peaceful and untroubled. But it wasn't right for him.

His intent wasn't to hurt her. He had wanted to take

her mind off being chased by Agent Brown. "You still might find that life, a husband and children, somewhere down the road."

She shrugged and looked off into the distance. "I don't think I could ever be that ordinary again. Not after Eric, not after all this."

They had walked some distance from the car when Diego noticed a dark sedan pulling into the lot. He thought it was their contact until Agent Brown stepped out.

They couldn't get back to their car. Agent Brown was only three parking spaces away from it. Diego scanned the park. Training had taught him it was smarter to stay in a crowd—but in this situation, he figured it was best to stay away from people. He didn't want a child to die at their expense. Agent Brown slammed his car door. He spotted them. Samantha's eyes went wild with fear. The agent shoved his hand into his suit jacket, probably reaching for his gun.

Diego tugged Samantha's sleeve. "This way, into the trees. We'll double back later."

They ran into the dense brush away from the trail. Agent Brown's head bobbed up over the tall bushes. He was close. They wouldn't be able to outrun him. Diego dived to the ground and hid behind some thick brush. Samantha pressed in beside him.

"How did he find us?" she whispered.

Diego shook his head, not wanting to make any noise. One of two things had happened. Others in the department could be involved. If not Lister, then whoever had been ordered to bring them in. Or there could be a tracking device in either his phone or the car, since both were

Bureau issued. He'd figure it out later. Right now, he needed to get them out of this park alive.

Two people on mountain bikes went by on the trail. The noise of his own breathing sounded as if it were on high volume. He pressed his stomach against the hard ground.

He heard footsteps. The brush was too thick to see anything clearly, but judging from the way the footsteps went fast, then slow and then stopped altogether, it was someone searching, not someone out for a jog.

The voice of a child broke through the silence. "Hey, what are you guys doing down there?"

Diego spun around. A boy of about five stood beside them, holding a kite. His head tilted to one side.

Samantha tensed, her gaze darting around.

Diego placed a finger over his lips to indicate to the child that he should be silent.

The little boy's face brightened. "Are you playing a game?"

Diego was terrified not only for them but for the kid. "You need to go now." He hoped his voice conveyed that this was serious. The little boy wrinkled his forehead and pursed his lips.

A female voice sounded through the trees. "Trevor, where are you?"

"Over here, Mom, talking to these people," he shouted.

Diego cringed.

A woman came to the edge of the forest. "Get over here right now, young man. Don't you wander off like that again."

With a backward glance at them, Trevor took off running toward his mother.

If Agent Brown had been anywhere close, he would

have heard the exchange. "We've got to go, *rapido*, now." Diego pushed himself to his feet and took off running.

He'd gone only a few paces when Samantha half screamed. The rest of her scream had been cut off by Agent Brown slapping a hand over her mouth and wrapping the other arm around her waist.

# TEN

Samantha watched as terror filled Diego's eyes when he swung around and saw them. Agent Brown let go of her waist, pulled out a gun and pressed it into Samantha's side. The pressure made it hard to take in a breath.

Diego didn't have a gun anymore. He must have left it at the office.

"Both of you had better come with me or she gets it here, right now."

Diego nodded.

"Walk in front of me. Keep your hands where I can see them. If you run, I'll shoot you and then shoot her."

She knew Diego wouldn't run. He wouldn't leave her to die. She only hoped he was coming up with a plan.

She could hear noises from the people in the park in the distance. Agent Brown must be taking them to a more secluded spot to kill them.

Her mind raced as she stared at Diego's back. There were two of them and only one of him, but he had the gun. They walked across a bridge. The sounds of the people in the park faded.

Agent Brown took his hand off her mouth and poked the gun in her back. "Keep going."

She caught a slight quick hand movement from Diego, an open palm. He was signaling for her to stop.

She planted her feet.

"Move," Agent Brown said.

The seconds stretched on for an eternity.

*Come on, Diego. What do you have in mind?*

Diego swung around and leaped through the air. Agent Brown aimed the gun at Diego. This was her chance. Head down, she crashed into their assailant like a battering ram. The shot went wild. Agent Brown fell backward into the stream, and she fell on top of him. The gun had a silencer on it. No one would be alerted by the sound.

Hands wrapped around her neck, and her vision filled with the angry red face of Agent Brown. Water soaked through her clothes as she twisted in an effort to get away. She struggled for breath, clawing at the agent's hands. Diego's face loomed behind Agent Brown's before striking the man on the back of his head. He let go of Samantha and dived after Diego. The two men landed blows on each other's faces and then Diego punched the other man hard in the stomach. Agent Brown doubled over.

"Run," Diego yelled.

She took off across the bridge, feet echoing on the wooden planks. She sprinted down the path, glancing over her shoulder. No Diego.

She ran faster. The scattered sounds of people enjoying the park grew louder. She scanned the faces as she headed toward the parking lot, hoping to spot the agents who were supposed to pick them up, but she couldn't find anyone who looked the part. She headed toward the car.

Diego had had the foresight to leave the keys in the ignition or maybe it was habit. In any case, she started the car up and pulled out of the space, waiting for Diego to emerge from the trees.

A few minutes passed. Tension knotted through her chest when she did not see him or Agent Brown.

She couldn't leave, not without Diego. A man honked his horn and she pulled forward. When she looked up, Agent Brown emerged from the trees.

Her breath caught as the agony seemed to coil around her stomach at the thought that he'd managed to kill her protector. *Not Diego. Please no.* The agent headed straight toward her car.

She pushed away the weight of sorrow that threatened to paralyze her and shifted into Drive. The passenger's-side door swung open. Diego jumped in beside her. Sweat dripped off his forehead and his clothes were wet.

Her face must have registered shock.

"What?" he said, offering her his sideways grin.

She opened her mouth to speak.

He pointed through the windshield at Agent Brown closing in on them. "Better hit it."

She pressed the gas and sped through the parking lot. Agent Brown arrived at his car just as she pulled out onto the street.

She stared straight ahead. "What happened? I thought for sure—"

"What? That he took me out? Come on. I'm like a cat," Diego said.

She was suddenly very angry with him. "Well, you're on your tenth life."

"Are you saying you would have missed me?" His tone was teasing despite the tension of the moment.

She shook her head. How could he be so cavalier? He must have nearly lost his life. "How did you get away?"

"I was sneaky in how I got back to the car."

She checked her rearview mirror. "He'll follow us, won't he?" She sped through the city street, taking an on-ramp.

His tone became serious as he looked over his shoulder. "The best thing to do is get into some heavy traffic. He won't be able to keep track of us." She checked the exit number coming up. Emerson Street should be busy this time of day.

Tension invaded her arms as she gripped the wheel and slipped into the long lines of vehicles. She wished Diego were doing the driving. He was so much better at this. Diego had bruises on his neck. "So did he almost kill you?"

"You don't need to know."

Up ahead the traffic light turned red. The cars were bumper to bumper.

"Talk to me about something so I won't be so nervous," she said.

He pulled out his phone. "I need to get rid of this, and we need to ditch the car as soon as possible."

This kind of talk was only going to make her more nervous. The light turned green. "Talk to me about something happy."

He thought for a moment. "I'll sing you the song my mother used to sing to me for bedtime when I was a boy. She sang to me and then we said prayers together every night until I was ten."

She tried to picture Diego as a little boy. "I'd like to hear it."

"It's in Spanish," he said.

"Sing it anyway."

She pressed the gas, moving with the flow of traffic.

Diego sang in a warm tenor voice. Her father had been a tenor. She had fond memories of him singing in church. The song was light and bouncy.

She relaxed a little.

Diego stopped singing. Even though she didn't speak Spanish, she knew the song had cut off rather than come to an end.

"He's behind us, isn't he?" She couldn't purge her voice of the terror that invaded every cell of her body. "I don't know if I can do this."

"You're doing fine." His voice was so calm. "Just keep moving. Stay in heavy traffic. He won't try anything with witnesses around, and he has to focus on his driving."

She checked the rearview mirror, but didn't see the dark sedan. "Where is he?"

"About three cars behind us in the same lane," Diego said.

The row of cars jerked forward. She pressed the gas. Her heart beat against her rib cage and sweat trickled down the back of her neck.

Diego's voice remained monotone, which helped her stay focused. "There's an exit coming up. You should take it, but you need to switch lanes very quickly and right before the exit, so he doesn't see it coming."

She saw the exit sign. She had a quarter mile to get through three lanes of traffic. "There's a hole in the lane next to me."

"Don't take it. He'll figure out what your plan is if you move over too soon. If you miss this exit, we'll catch the next one. The important thing is you need to surprise him."

She took in a breath, studied the gaps in the stream of cars and calculated the fastest way to the exit. She waited until they were within seconds of the off-ramp before slipping into the next lane of traffic and then the second.

"Did he follow us?"

Diego craned his neck and checked the rearview mirror. "Looks like we're clear."

Joy surged through her for what she'd been able to accomplish. "Well, how about that."

"Yeah, how about that, *chica*." Diego grinned and shook his head.

"So, what do we do now?" She hoped he had some kind of plan. They seemed safe at the moment—but the past few days had taught her that safety didn't tend to last very long.

That was a question that had plagued him ever since he realized Agent Brown was involved. "We can't go back to the agency. Not until I know who else is working with Agent Brown."

He checked his mirrors and studied the street in front of him. If this was about Diego's work to undermine the gang's drug network, then Agent Brown had a whole army at his disposal, in addition to whatever agents he'd been able to turn. "There is only one agent I would trust with my life."

She sat back in the seat. "Who's that?"

"Gabriel Tovar came up on the street with me. He's the one who talked me into being a CI after he joined the Bureau."

"The Bureau. You mean the FBI? That's who you work for? We should call him," she said.

He didn't mind letting it slip that his work was with the FBI. She'd probably figured most of it out anyway.

"Gabriel's out of the country dealing with an international situation."

She took a moment to respond. "Can't we just go to the local cops?"

"Our story wouldn't sound believable. There'd be too many holes. I can't tell them everything—a lot of my work is still classified. I'm not allowed to tell anyone without special clearance until criminal proceedings are complete." He knew he could trust her with the whole story, but it wasn't his call to make.

"So we wait until your friend Gabriel gets back?" she asked, her words weighted with frustration.

"We can't wait that long. It's not just Agent Brown we have to worry about. Word has probably gone out to look for a dark-haired man and blonde woman." At least he knew the neighborhoods where the Piru gang had most of their activity. He could at least avoid that pitfall.

"We should change how we look, then," she said.

"For someone who grew up in the burbs, you have pretty good survival skills."

"You'd be surprised. It's not all mansions and tea parties," she said, offering him a coy smile.

She drove around until she located a neighborhood drugstore.

As always, when they got out of the car, he studied each person on the street. The kids loitering outside the coffee shop, the older couple buying a newspaper and the twenty-something man standing off by himself.

The gang members, drug dealers and rogue agents couldn't be everywhere at once. If anything, he should watch the cars that parked and who got out of them.

"We need to ditch this car, too," he said. "Even if it doesn't have some sort of tracking device, it's so obviously an agency car." He threw his phone in the garbage can.

They walked the aisle of the drugstore together, grabbing two hats and two new hoodies and a T-shirt for Samantha. After they made their purchases, they walked to a park that was ten minutes from the drugstore.

"If you want, you can change in there." He pointed toward the restroom. "I don't think anyone will bother you. I'll keep watch outside."

She nodded, her eyes filled with trust. "Thanks for sticking with me."

"Why wouldn't I?" He touched her cheek lightly.

Her expression softened. He wanted to kiss her. He leaned a little closer. She cast her gaze downward and he knew he'd been out of line.

"Diego, what are we going to do next until your friend gets back? How does this play out?"

Upset with himself for trying to kiss her, he took a step back. He knew they needed help, but it had to be a source he could trust. "We need to borrow a car. Is there anyone from your old neighborhood who could loan us one?"

"No. Maybe somebody from Evergreen Catering could." The question seemed to upset her. She turned and disappeared into the bathroom.

Diego stood by the door, watching the activity in the park. A mom with a little girl eyed him suspiciously before entering the bathroom.

If he wasn't concerned about keeping Samantha safe, he'd go back to the neighborhoods he'd been working and see if he could find out the connection back to the Bureau from that angle. Diego took off the hoodie he'd bought on the boat, tossed it in the trash can and put on the new lime green one he'd grabbed at the drugstore. Now he wished he'd thought to get a disposable phone, as well.

As he waited for Samantha and watched the sun slowly setting, he was uncertain of what their next move was. The only thing he knew for sure was that he had to keep Samantha safe. They might come from different worlds, but she'd become important to him, all the same.

With nowhere else to turn, all he could think to do was pray.

*God, please don't let me let her down.*

# ELEVEN

Samantha placed the baseball hat on her head and looked at herself in the dirty mirror.

Diego's question about who she could call for help had upset her. Just a reminder of how disconnected from her old life she was. And in her new life, she didn't really have any close connections. The people at Evergreen Catering were nice, but she had been deliberate in keeping the relationships distant. Even Elise didn't know anything of her past.

The door swung open and she jumped. It was just a mother and little girl using the toilet. She waited for her heart to slow down.

From the bathroom stall, she could hear the mother patiently answering all her daughter's questions. Samantha had only a vague memory of her own mother. Her father had done his best to fill in the blanks, share photographs and memories with her. But none of that replaced hugs and a patient voice explaining the world to you.

Still waiting for the mom and little girl to finish, she stepped into a bathroom stall and slipped Diego's sweater off. Feeling the rough texture of the wool on her palm reminded her of Diego. She brought the sweater up to her face and breathed in. It still smelled like him, a little. She put on the T-shirt and hoodie they'd purchased at the drugstore. She heard the outside door open and ease shut. The mom and child must have left.

She stepped out into the evening light. Diego pushed himself off the swing set he'd been leaning against.

"Hello there, stranger." His eyes were bright and his smile warmed her clean through.

She touched the side of her head. "So do I look like a whole new person?"

"You look less like you." He tugged on a strand of her hair. "Why don't you let me braid it? Your long flowing hair makes you easier to spot."

"You know how to braid hair?"

"I had two sisters and a mom who had to work two jobs," he said.

She took off her baseball hat, wandered over to the swings and sat down. He ran his palm over her hair. "It's a little tangled. I'll comb through it with my fingers. If you're all right with that?"

"Sure," she whispered.

She felt only a gentle tug as he finger-combed her hair, then braided it. His fingers brushed the back of her neck. Her heart fluttered at his touch, but she shook off the feelings of attraction. She trusted Diego, but she still didn't trust where attraction might lead.

Earlier she'd thought that Diego might kiss her. Even that scared her. He probably only felt a strong connection to her because of the desperation of their situation.

"There." He squeezed her shoulder. "Turn around. Let me see."

She pushed herself out of the swing and turned to face him.

He nodded his approval. "You don't look anything like yourself."

"I suppose that was the goal." She felt a tightening in her throat as she asked the next question. "What do we do now?"

He took in a breath. "We go back to my old neighborhood. There are people there who can help us."

"Okay, let's do that, then," she said.

His lips formed a tight, hard line. "We'll have to go through a neighborhood that could be dangerous."

Though she could guess at what his work was about, and why it put him at risk, she wished she knew more. "I know you can't explain why to me."

"Just know that it's connected with the gangs there and the drug dealing. And what I have been doing can make a difference in a good way." His voice filled with passion.

"Okay, if that is what we have to do." Even as she spoke, she could feel the fear rising up.

"Good. Then there is a bus we can catch a couple of streets from here," he said.

They walked across the park as the evening sky turned from gray to charcoal. When they got to the bus stop, one other person, an older African-American woman, was waiting.

She scooted over on the bench so Samantha could sit.

"Last bus of the day," the woman said with a heavy sigh.

Samantha nodded. Diego continued to pace and watch the street.

"This is a beautiful time of night." The older woman tilted her head toward the sky. "God does some of His best work at this hour."

Somewhere in the distance, Samantha detected the noises of a basketball game, the bouncing of the ball on concrete and the sound of young men taking verbal jabs at each other. The air was chilled but not cold.

Diego stopped pacing and stared at the older woman and then nodded as he gazed at the setting sun. "Yes, He does."

"You might be right about that." A joy came over Samantha that she didn't understand. She didn't know this woman's story. Maybe she was headed home after a long day of work at a less-than-wonderful job, but she had taken a moment to see God in the middle of all of it. She wished she could do that.

The bus came to a stop and they got on. There were no seats available for them to sit together. He directed Samantha to sit with a forty-something woman in a shabby coat. He found a place farther back.

She felt exposed and vulnerable without Diego by her side. She studied the people around her. A teenager with tattoos on his neck gave her a hard stare that sent chills through her.

Why was her response so fearful? She bent her head and stared at the floor. There was no reason to think he knew who she was. It was good that she and Diego weren't sitting together. They were less likely to be identified.

The bus rolled for several blocks and came to a stop. Four people rose and made their way to the front. Samantha felt a squeeze on her arm just above the elbow. Diego pressed close to her.

"We need to go."

She hurried toward the front of the bus. This couldn't be the stop he wanted.

He leaned close to her. "When we got on, one of the men made a phone call when he saw us. I only picked up a few words, but the way he kept looking at me... We can't take a chance."

When they exited the bus, she saw several men standing by the stop. Thankfully, they didn't pay any attention to her or Diego. She glanced up into the bus windows where she spotted the teenager from before glaring at her.

Diego led her through the city streets to a bar. The bar was filled with people and loud music. The smells and the noise assaulted her senses. He stopped to whisper something into the ear of one of the other patrons before leading her to a back room that was quiet.

"Wait here," he said.

"Where are you going?"

"I'm going to try to get us a car or at least a phone. Be careful. This is enemy territory. And I don't know who I can trust and who knows what." It was the first time she'd heard fear in his voice.

Panic settled around her like a heavy Seattle rain. "Diego?"

"You don't need to see any of this. I'll be back for you."

"And if you're not?"

"Haven't I kept my word so far?"

She had a feeling there were factors he couldn't control in this situation. "Yes, yes, you have." She would trust him.

"Just stay here until I get back."

He closed the door. The booming music seemed to make the walls pulsate. She was in some sort of storage/break room that consisted of two chairs and shelves filled with cleaning supplies and plastic cups. She laced her fingers together and a trickle of sweat snaked down her back.

Someone slammed hard against the outside wall. She

jumped out of the chair as the tension formed a hard rock in her stomach. She eased back down on the chair.

*He said to wait.*

She'd counted the beats of music to over a hundred when the door burst open.

Diego's face was flushed. "I got us a car. Let's go. It's a few blocks up this street."

He grabbed her hand and led her to a back parking lot. Just as they were about to leave the parking lot, a voice called to them from the darkness.

"Hey, dog." A large Hispanic man stepped out into the light. His eyes raked over Samantha in a way that made her uncomfortable. "This is your new *chica*, no? *Ella es caliente.*" His voice held a tone of menace as he loomed toward them.

Before her eyes, she saw Diego become a different person. His posture and his voice changed. He said something in Spanish. The inflection of his voice suggested that what he said was salacious. Only the comfort of his palm resting on the middle of her back told her that he was acting a part. The touch was meant to reassure her while he continued his lewd conversation.

The two men shook hands and patted each other on the back. The last thing the stranger said was in Spanish, but it sounded like a warning. The big man took a step back and disappeared, engulfed in the darkness.

"I didn't want you to see that." In the dark, his face was very close to hers.

She tilted her head. "I understand that you have to become someone else to do the work you do."

He lingered there, his cheek touching hers. "It's somebody I don't like."

"You do it to make a difference, to make the world a

better, safer place, right?" she whispered. He stood so close to her she could feel his body heat.

"I'm glad you understand." His lips found hers and brushed lightly over them, causing a warm radiance all over her skin. She leaned closer, placing her palm on his chest, feeling his heart pound, wishing the moment could last longer.

He pulled away. His head went up, but in the dark she couldn't see his eyes.

He stepped toward the sidewalk. "I got this car from a low-level drug dealer who owed me a favor. I don't think he has high enough connections to do me any harm." Diego was all business as though the kiss had not taken place.

She wondered if the guy in the parking lot would get the word out that he'd seen them. As they stepped out into the lit street, her fingers brushed over Diego's arm and he responded by dropping his head and smiling coyly. Enough for her to know the kiss meant something to him, too.

"The car is just a little way up this street." They stepped into an alley. Though there were noises in the distance— music, people shouting, cars roaring to life—the alley was quiet.

A car squealed to a stop, blocking their exit from the alley. Another one appeared on the other end. The cars idled with their lights on.

"This way." Diego pointed up the fire escape.

As they climbed, a dark figure got out of each car and raced toward them. One of them grabbed Diego's foot, pulling him back down to the ground. The men started throwing punches. Samantha grabbed a potted plant from the stoop she was on. Diego delivered a hard left hook to one of the men, sending him to the ground. He whirled around and threw a punch at the second attacker just as he was about to jump on Diego.

Samantha waited until Diego separated from the second man before dropping the plant. Her missile hit its target. The attacker crumpled to the ground. The first man pulled himself to his feet as Diego climbed toward Samantha. They sprinted across the rooftop.

She glanced over her shoulder. One of the men had made it to the roof. Diego stopped at the edge of the roof at another fire escape. "One more block over." He climbed down first. "The other one might be waiting for us."

She made it three rungs down the fire escape when a hand grabbed her wrist from above. She saw a man's face, all teeth and forehead. The man pulled her up toward him. His face loomed larger until she could see the pockmarks on his cheeks and smell his sour breath. Diego held on to her legs, pulling her downward. She turned her head and sank her teeth into the assailant's hand. He yowled and let go of her wrists. Samantha tumbled down to the landing. Diego grabbed her, wrapping his arms around her waist. She whirled around, clutching his chest.

The attacker was halfway down the ladder. They clambered to the edge of the landing. She climbed down first, jumping free of the ladder midway. Diego was right behind her. On the ground, Diego took the lead, racing through the apartment building's parking lot.

He ran one way and then the other. She followed him, pushing down the rising panic. Was the car not where it was supposed to be?

The first attacker had just rounded the corner of the building, and the second one had nearly climbed down the last section of ladders.

Diego stopped and waved her over. He ran toward a car, dived in, started it up and gunned the engine. Both men were closing in on her as she grabbed the passenger's-side door handle. She landed in the seat and slammed the door as the car sped up.

He hit the blinker and turned out onto the dark street. "I think we'll take the long way back to my old neighborhood just to make sure we're not followed."

"Where did those men come from?"

"They were low-level thugs that somebody dug up last minute. They didn't even have guns." He let out a heavy breath. "Word is out on the street about me."

He turned out onto the freeway. The lights of the city shone like glitter on a Christmas tree. As the minutes ticked by, her muscles relaxed and she took in a breath.

Diego turned off onto an exit. "I cut all ties with this neighborhood when I went undercover. I didn't want anyone I cared about to end up hurt because of me." He drove past dark storefronts until he came to a park by a lakefront. "You hungry?" He pointed toward an all-night food truck.

"Starving," she said.

He pulled the car over and got out. Samantha watched through the windshield, wondering how much longer this game of cat and mouse would go on.

# TWELVE

Diego ordered two burgers with fries. The cook and the female clerk bantered with each other while the hamburger patties sizzled on the grill. Their conversation moved back and forth between Spanish and English. The sound relaxed him. He was home. One of his sisters lived five blocks from here.

The thought brought a mixture of relief and anxiety. Relief because it was always good to come back to where he'd grown up. Anxiety because he knew that if Agent Brown or anyone in collusion with him got wind of where they were, he'd be putting the people he cared about at risk. His back was against a wall. Until Gabriel made contact, he needed a place to hide.

"Here you go, sir." The clerk pushed two greasy containers toward him. She was an older woman with a tattoo of a cross on her forearm and a nose ring. "You look familiar."

He studied the woman closer, but shook his head.

The woman pointed a finger at him, recognition spreading across her face. "Carmen's boy."

The mention of his mother's name was like a knife stab to his heart.

The woman rested a hand on her hip. "Little Diego, all grown up."

Diego blushed, feeling as if he were twelve years old again.

"I owned the bakery down on S. Austin Street for over ten years." The woman narrowed her eyes. "What brings you back to the neighborhood?"

"Just a visit to see my sister Claudia." No one but his sisters knew about his work. To everyone in the old neighborhood, Diego was still a gang member.

"Oh, yes. She's still there. Those boys of hers are getting so big. They'll be glad to see their uncle."

Again, that slicing feeling through his heart at what he'd given up. Though it was a different neighborhood and different gang territory, he'd always hoped that what he chose to do made the whole city safer for those he loved.

He returned to the car and handed Samantha the food. He took a few bites of his burger, letting the flavor explode in his mouth. Samantha munched on her fries and dabbed her chin with the paper napkin.

"We'll be going to my sister's house." He hoped it wouldn't spook her too badly. When he did make contact with his sister, it was always at the hospital where she was a nurse. "The way I got it figured, I can purchase a gun using some old contacts. I'll send Claudia to buy us a phone. We'll get some sleep and be out of this neighborhood in less than five hours. Maybe by then we'll hear from Gabriel."

She set her burger down and turned to face him. "You mean it's not safe here."

"It's safer than anywhere else I can think of. The gangs tend to stay in their own territory, but there is always spillover, and I can't risk that somebody here might be talking to someone elsewhere."

Her mouth stretched into a tight line. Then she turned away and stared out the window.

"I wish I could say it was totally safe, but that would be a lie."

"It's all right." Her voice was soft, drifting to some faraway place.

He hated putting her through all this. "I know you're tired." He started up the car and drove through the neighborhood. Only a few of the windows still had lights on.

Once he parked the car, Diego focused on one lit window. "That's my sister. She's studying for a master's in nursing. She could work at any hospital, but she chooses to stay here."

Samantha beamed. "You're pretty proud of her."

"Yeah, I am." He got out of the car and strode through the courtyard. In the distance, he heard gunfire and a few seconds later a siren. Nothing new to him, but Samantha pressed a little closer to him. He wrapped his arms around her, remembering their brief kiss. Chances were it would be the only one. His life, the mission he needed to complete, was just too crazy to bring her into it.

They took the interior stairs to the second floor. Diego paused before knocking. Footsteps pounded across the floor and then the door swung open. Claudia's expression transformed from happy when she looked at Diego to surprised when she noticed Samantha.

Then she drew her eyebrows together. "*Oye manito,* what's up?"

"I need your help," Diego said. "We won't be here long."

She nodded and stepped aside. His sister didn't need to ask questions. She knew from the tone of his voice that it was serious. She understood why he had chosen the life he had.

His nephew Tomas slept on the couch like he always did. His other nephew, Jerome, was probably asleep in the next room. David, Claudia's husband, worked nights at the hospital.

"I hope I haven't brought the lion to your door," Diego said.

"David and I can handle the lion. We always have. Both my boys have stayed out of trouble despite it being all around them." She tilted her head toward the teenager sleeping on the couch. "What do you need me to do, *manito*?"

"I need a prepaid phone."

Claudia reached for her coat, which was slung over the back of a chair. "Jiffy's is open all night. It won't take me long." She planted a kiss on her brother's cheek before leaving. "As always, it's good to see you even if it's only for a short time."

She left, closing the door behind her.

Samantha looked around the clean but sparse apartment. Was it hitting her just how poor he'd been growing up? The contrast between their lives had to be becoming even more evident.

She wandered over to a wall where Claudia had hung photos of him, their other sister, their mother and her own children.

She turned around to face Diego. "A family lives here." Her voice filled with appreciation.

He liked her even more in that moment. She saw what really mattered. Why was he so fixated on their different upbringings when she wasn't?

He gathered her into his arms. "Thank you." She melted

against him. He buried his face in her hair, relishing having her close.

"A family is a precious thing," she said.

He pulled away from her and gathered a pillow from an armchair, tossing it on the floor. "Sorry, there are no extra beds, but you can get some sleep on the carpet. I'll wake you when it's time to go."

She lay down on her side, drawing her knees up toward her stomach. He rummaged through a hall closet and got a blanket, then laid it over her carefully.

She spoke to him with her eyes closed. "Aren't you going to sleep?"

"Soon as my sister gets back with that phone, I'm going to make some calls, try to round up a gun."

He settled in an armchair and watched out the window, waiting for his sister's headlights to cast shadows on the wall. The stiffness left Samantha's body and her breathing deepened. His nephew snored from the couch.

Against his better wishes, he closed his own eyes and the heaviness of sleep overtook him.

Samantha awoke with the soft blanket snug around her shoulders. She heard panting. When she turned her head to the side, a boy of about ten and a small dog stared at her from the couch. The boy on the couch last night had been a teenager.

"You must be Diego's other nephew."

"I'm Jerome." The boy nodded. "This is Lassie." He pointed to the dog who was not remotely a collie. The dog was a small, scruffy mutt, some sort of poodle-terrier mix.

"Nice name," Samantha said.

"I read it in a book. My mom makes me read a lot."

Samantha sat up and rubbed her eyes. "That's not a bad thing."

"She says if I have a book, I'll never be lonely or bored." Jerome petted Lassie. "I think that's true about dogs, too."

"Your mom is very wise." She looked around. "Where's Diego?"

"Outside playing B-ball. He said I was supposed to make you toast when you woke up." The boy jumped to his feet with the dog trailing after him.

While Jerome pulled bread out of the bag and stuffed it in the toaster, Samantha rose to her feet and peered out the window. Down below in the parking lot, Diego dribbled a basketball and tossed it through a makeshift basket that had been attached to an electrical pole.

Jerome brought over a piece of toast on a plate. "I put butter on it."

She stared down at the round cherub face and the scruffy dog sitting at his feet looking up at her with the same expression of expectation.

"Thank you," she said. "This looks delicious."

She opened the window and nibbled on her toast while listening to the sound of the basketball game, the supportive slaps on the back the boys gave each other as well as the verbal jousting. The respectful way they looked to Diego when a foul was called. He seemed to have a talent for drawing every boy in. It was the first time she'd seen Diego totally relaxed.

When a siren sounded in the distance, she wasn't alarmed. She'd heard them throughout the night. Her back stiffened, though, when the siren grew louder and closer and then a police car pulled into the lot where the basketball game was happening. The two officers walked toward Diego and began to talk to him. Something about their body language said that this was not going to end well.

She raced down the stairs. By the time she got outside, they had Diego in handcuffs.

"What's going on here?"

"We're taking him in on trying to obtain a gun illegally."

Diego leaned toward her. "It's not true. This is a setup. You got to get me out of jail as fast as you can. I don't think I'll live very long if you don't. There are always plenty of gang members in holding, and it would be easy for an 'accident' to happen to me."

As they dragged Diego away, Samantha felt as though a cord were twisting around her middle, growing tighter and tighter.

One of the boys stood next to her, turning the basketball in his hand. "He's innocent, man. Diego's a good guy."

She watched the police car pull away from the curb. Her mind raced in a thousand directions at once.

"How am I going to get him out of jail?" she asked, speaking mostly to herself.

"Gotta make bail." Another boy came up beside her.

The first boy dribbled the ball and then tossed it to his friend. "They can hold him for twenty-four hours without charging him."

"Bail," she repeated. "Money."

Jerome came toward her holding a phone. "I called my mom at the hospital."

Claudia's voice sounded unnerved. "Samantha, Jerome just told me what happened."

Samantha struggled to get the words out. "Diego

thinks he's been set up. That someone might try to kill him in jail."

"I will make some phone calls to see if we can make bail. You need to get down to the jail, see if you can talk to Diego. Find out what is going on. My older son, Tomas, has a car. He can drive you there."

"Okay. I don't have a phone. Can I take this one?"

"Sure. It belongs to Tomas. He'll survive without it."

Samantha felt numb as Diego's teenage nephew drove her across town to the police station. She thanked Tomas for the ride and made her way up the wide concrete steps. The police station bustled with activity. Officers sat in their carrels typing at computers. Others milled around visiting with each other or grabbing police-issue duffels and heading out the door. The calls coming in from dispatch made up the background noise. There was no sign of Diego. The criminals must be processed in a separate part of the building.

A tall, thin man behind a counter just inside the door seemed to be the one directing traffic in and out of the station.

"Excuse me." Samantha approached the counter. The thin man made eye contact with her and then turned around and yelled at an officer leaning on a file cabinet. "Knutsen, you were supposed to pick up your perp out of holding ten minutes ago."

Officer Knutsen rolled his eyes. "Got distracted." He disappeared through a door at the back of the station. That door must lead to the jail.

"Yes, can I help you?" The man came across as abrupt and demanding.

She was already frightened and confused. His demeanor flustered her. "I…um… They arrested a man, Diego Cruz… I need to see him."

"How long ago was he brought in?"

"Less than half an hour ago," she said.

"He's probably still in processing. You can see him once he's in his cell. Are you a family member?"

"No, I'm…a friend," she said.

"Only his lawyer and family can see him."

"I know his sister." She took her borrowed phone out and stared at it. Claudia probably wouldn't be able to come until her shift at the hospital ended. "How soon is the next bail hearing?"

"There is one scheduled for nine o'clock tomorrow."

That meant Diego would be held in the jail for at least twenty-four hours, longer if they couldn't make the bail.

"Diego thinks he might be in some danger. That someone might try to hurt him while he's in jail."

"Don't they all." The tall man's phone rang. He lifted the receiver and turned away from Samantha.

She had to talk to Diego. Waiting until Claudia got here might be too late. Samantha slipped past the counter while the desk sergeant's attention was diverted. She opened the door where Officer Knutsen had gone and found herself in a lobby space that had a list of offices and a map. Processing was down the hallway and to the right. She made her way down the hallway and pushed open a door.

She stepped out onto a balcony with a glass wall. Down below, she saw uniformed officers fingerprinting men and women. Some of the criminals were cuffed and escorted by officers; others waited in line to be printed and photographed. Two people, a man and woman, dressed in suits occupied the balcony with her. Their conversation was low and hushed, but she gathered from the legal-sounding words that the two were attorneys.

She edged a little closer to them when there was a gap in their conversation. "Can anyone go down there?"

The female lawyer tugged on the hem of her blazer. "Only the lucky few who are being charged with something."

She scanned the area, until she saw Diego cuffed and sitting at a desk while an officer asked him questions.

He tilted his head up as though he sensed her staring. She laid her palm on the glass.

The female lawyer stepped a little closer. "It's one-way glass. They can't see you. Is someone you love down there?"

"Love…ah…no…ah." She could feel her cheeks heat up. "Someone who has helped me out…a great deal." The woman had kind eyes. "You're a lawyer, right?"

The woman nodded.

"How much is bail going to be for someone who is charged with trying to illegally obtain a gun?"

The lady lawyer looked over at her colleague. "What do you think?"

The man shrugged. "I'd guess under five thousand if he's not a flight risk and isn't a career criminal."

Samantha wasn't sure what to do. People seemed to be coming and going pretty freely in the processing area. All the security gates were for people coming from outside on the street.

The two lawyers slipped away. She was left alone on the viewing platform. The officer led Diego over to the fingerprinting area, where the officer undid Diego's handcuffs but remained close to him.

Samantha watched the movement of the other people

on the floor. One man in particular seemed to be on a mission. It was his brisk walk that caught her eye. He slowed suddenly as though he didn't want to call attention to himself. The man scanned the entire area, searching for something or someone.

Samantha leaned a little closer to the glass. Her breath caught when she saw the man check the inside of his coat pocket, indicating he had something hidden there—a weapon, maybe? All the air whooshed out of her lungs when the man spotted Diego and made a beeline for him.

# THIRTEEN

Diego turned his head slightly. He sensed that he was being watched.

"No fast moves," said the officer standing next to him. "Put your finger on the ink pad."

Instincts honed from his days on the street told him he was under threat. The hairs on the back of his neck stood up. He felt that heated prickling of his skin that told him danger was close by. As he went through the motions for fingerprinting, he separated out the different sounds in the processing room. Low mumbling, papers being shuffled, fingers tapping keyboards. Then he heard it. Footsteps moving at a rapid pace and growing closer.

He whirled around, scanning the crowd.

"Hey." The officer fingerprinting him gripped Diego's upper arm.

It took him less than a second to lock on to the menace on the face of the dark-haired man approaching him. Though he slowed his pace when Diego spotted him, his intentions were obvious.

The officer squeezed Diego's arm. "Face forward."

Reluctantly, Diego took his eyes off his would-be attacker. Maybe Diego's glare had been enough to ward him off. He'd lost the element of surprise.

"You might want to check out the guy in the red shirt," Diego said to the officer.

"Let's just get through this," said the officer.

He couldn't see the man out of his peripheral vision.

The crowd of people seemed to draw closer to him. A woman a few feet away from him screamed. He felt a sting across his upper arm where a sharp object plunged into his biceps. His body went into shock as he reached out for his assailant, who held a jagged piece of metal.

The officer grabbed him and pushed him back against a wall. Blood gushed from his arm. The cut was deep. He saw black spots around the edges of his vision.

Then Samantha's face popped into view. Her lovely blue eyes reflected his own fear. "I saw. I got down here as fast as I could."

The crowd whirred and mumbled around him. Another woman gasped in a way that sounded more like a soft scream. He slipped in and out of consciousness as he was lifted onto something and moved through space on his back. Ceiling tiles clipped by.

A hand slipped into his. And he heard her voice again. "I'm here, Diego."

He was aware that he was being wheeled somewhere, but his strongest impression was of the softness of her hand in his.

He slipped into unconsciousness. When he woke up in a hospital bed, Samantha was sitting beside him.

He felt light-headed. He stared down at the bandage on his upper arm.

"It was a pretty deep gash, but it'll heal. He was aiming for your heart." She leaned toward him and twisted a corner of the bedsheet in her fingers. "I guess the fact that he missed is the good news."

He stared at his surroundings. The room was small and without windows.

"It's the infirmary in the jail. They said you could stay here until your bail hearing tomorrow morning. Now they believe me that your life is at risk, so they let me see you even though I'm not family."

That was a good turn of events. "What kind of security do they have here?"

"They said they would post a guard outside the door."

He nodded. He sat up a little higher. Samantha jumped to her feet to adjust his pillow. Her hand brushed the back of his neck.

Pain sliced up his arm. "I got it." He sounded defensive. He watched her deflate before his eyes.

"Sorry, stupid Latino pride," he said.

She cast her gaze downward and spoke in a low voice. "Well, they said I could only stay until you woke up."

He wondered if that was true or if she was trying to make a graceful exit after he'd snapped at her.

"I'll be at the bail hearing tomorrow," she said.

"Agent Brown must have set this up. We need to get out of here as quickly as possible. By now everyone who wants me dead knows where I am."

"I will have the car waiting," she said. "Maybe your friend Gabriel will be back by then."

"Have we made bail?"

"I don't know yet. I need to talk to your sister. I have to go." She leaned forward as though to kiss him on the forehead but then thought better of it and straightened her back. "I'll see you tomorrow."

He wrapped his hand around her wrist. "I'm sorry for snapping at you."

She patted his shoulder. "It's all right. It's just been a really long day."

His eyes searched hers. "Thank you for coming for me when you did."

"I was on the viewing platform." The temperature in the room seemed to drop. "Diego, I saw you…" Her eyes glazed. "I saw him coming for you and I…" She cupped her hand over her mouth as she turned away and left the room.

A heaviness settled around him. Despite his best effort, he and Samantha had bonded. It was clear from the way the thought of his death had affected her.

And he was affected just as badly. Because even injured, in a prison infirmary, all he could think about was that she was out there on dangerous streets tonight, without his protection.

Distraught, Samantha hurried down the hall. She'd watched Diego almost die. Nearly losing him made her realize how much she cared about him. What was going to happen to them when all this was over? If they made it out alive.

Her phone rang. The screen on Tomas's phone told her the call was from Mom… Claudia.

She pressed the connect button and cleared her throat to hide that she'd been crying.

"Yes."

"Are you all right? How is it going with Diego?"

With only one word Claudia had been able to figure out all was not well.

"There was an incident in processing. Diego ended up in the infirmary."

Claudia said something in Spanish that sounded fearful.

"He's going to be okay, and he's actually safer where he's at now," Samantha said.

There was a long pause before Claudia said anything. "The reason why I called was that I wanted to let you know that the den mothers—that's what the women at the church who pray for the community are called—raised two thousand dollars."

Samantha's heart was touched when she pictured mothers and children emptying their piggy banks and pocketbooks. "A lawyer I talked to thought it might be closer to five thousand."

"Oh." Claudia sounded deflated.

They *had* to make bail. Diego would be killed if he remained in jail. "There is something I might be able to do. I might be able to come up with some money."

"Okay," said Claudia with a little hesitation. "Tomas will be around to pick you up in just a few minutes. Wait inside the building. He'll call when he gets there."

"Thanks, Claudia."

"Samantha, I'm really worried about Diego." Claudia's usually strong voice faltered.

"Me, too." She hung up and found a quiet alcove where she would be able to make her phone call. She stared down at the phone for a long time. She did not have any money to speak of, but she knew people who did. She knew Alisha's number by heart. They had grown up together in Cambridge Heights. Contacting her, though, meant that Eric might find out where she was. She punched in the number. It was a risk she was willing to take for Diego.

The phone rang three times before anyone picked up. "Hello."

She recognized her friend's clear, sweet voice.

"Alisha."

"Sam, is that you?"

Eric had poisoned everyone against her, but Alisha didn't sound at all guarded. Samantha's throat went tight. She was having a hard time finding words.

"It's good to hear your voice," said Alisha. "I didn't know if I ever would again."

"How is everything there?"

Alisha let out a heavy breath. "I owe you an apology. You told me Eric was bad news. I should have believed you."

Samantha felt as though she finally had air in her lungs after holding her breath for a very long time. "Thank you."

"I don't know exactly what is going on, but Eric was working some kind of business deal with Nelson Stride across the street. Nelson totally lost his shirt, and he says Eric cheated him. I don't understand the whole thing, but anyway, I don't think Eric is going to be living here much longer."

"But he is still there…in the house my father bought for us?"

"Yes, he's still here." Alisha sounded as though she was talking through gritted teeth. "Are you— Can you come back? Where have you been for the past year, anyway?"

"I can't get into that right now. Alisha, I need your help."

"Of course." Her friend's response was without hesitation.

"It's really important that Eric doesn't find out that I called you."

This time Alisha paused before answering. "Okay… sure."

"I need to know if I can borrow three thousand dollars from you." The money, enough to save Diego's life, would be a drop in the bucket to Alisha. She had family money and her husband had done well as an investment banker.

"Sure. I can do that," Alisha said.

"It would be a loan. I can pay you back over time."

"No need. Consider it a gift, my way of apologizing for not believing you," Alisha said.

Samantha's heart warmed. "Thanks, Alisha. I'll get back to you with the account information to transfer the money."

"It's good to hear your voice. Wish I could see you again. Give you a hug."

The emotion in her friend's words touched her. It had been so long since she'd felt accepted by the people she had known all her life. But now it sounded as if Eric was slowly revealing his true colors to the other people in the neighborhood and would soon be gone. She hadn't ever thought she'd be able to return to her childhood home. "Maybe sometime in the future, I could see you. Please remember what I said about not telling anyone." She thanked her friend and hung up.

Her phone buzzed and a text came up on her screen. I'm waiting outside. Tomas.

She stepped outside beneath an overcast sky and headed toward Tomas's car. She had the feeling it was going to be a long night.

To Diego's surprise, the night in the infirmary and the bail hearing went off without incident. The property clerk returned the few personal belongings he had had when he was arrested, and he headed up to where Samantha waited for him in the lobby of the justice center.

She was wearing a pink blouse, jeans and a jacket that he recognized as belonging to his sister. He regretted that he wouldn't have a chance to say goodbye to Claudia and his nephews, but it would be safer for everyone this way. The brightness of Samantha's smile warmed him through to the bone.

"You ready to go?" she said. "The car is waiting. There wasn't any street parking. I had to park in the parking garage."

Less safe, but he couldn't change it. Rain drizzled from the sky. Once inside, their footsteps echoed inside the parking garage. Word was probably getting back to Agent Brown that he'd made bail. He half expected to be shot at in the parking garage.

She walked beside him. "I did manage to find a spot on the second floor."

They arrived at the car and got in. As he turned the wheel, his arm stung from the gash. He pulled out of the space when he heard a thump on the trunk. A man, clearly a gang member, had hit the car with his fist. Another man and a tall woman came out of the shadows and began to beat on the hood of the car.

He saw the terror in Samantha's eyes.

"They're intimidating us, that's all."

Another man came out of the darkness and tapped on Samantha's window with his knuckles.

She drew back. "Are you sure about that?"

He backed up slowly as the pounding continued. "If they wanted to kill us, they would have by now. These are some low-level thugs willing to do this for a little cash. They're probably not even armed."

Diego knew what the top-down message was. Agent Brown or whoever controlled the operation from the inside wanted him to know he and Samantha were being watched, and that it was just a matter of time before they were killed.

When he got the car turned around, he hit the gas, leaving the band of intimidators behind. He sped out onto the street.

"How much longer until Gabriel gets back?"

"I'm not sure. He should have been back by now, but an investigation isn't like a business trip—it doesn't have a scheduled end date. He'll get back into the country when he finds what he needs to find. He hasn't responded to my text. I know if he was able to communicate, he would."

"Could we try one more time?"

Gabriel was their last hope for getting this thing resolved without stirring the hornet's nest again.

He handed her the phone and recited the number to her, which he knew by heart. "When you send the text, call him Ricky."

"You said his name was Gabriel."

"It's just a precaution in case the phone falls into the wrong hands."

She shook her head. "Very James Bond."

He shook his head. His life was nothing like the fictional British spy's. He saw the darkest part of humanity and tried not to be overtaken by it. "When you send the text, don't be specific. Just ask him if he's done with his previous engagement."

She sent the text and then stared out at the passing landscape. "That's my old high school."

She'd gone to school less than twenty blocks from where he'd grown up.

Diego glanced at the school. "I remember when students from there would come into our neighborhood to clean it up, paint over the graffiti and stuff, some sort of community project."

"I remember doing that. How did that make you feel when we showed up?"

"Like a bug in a glass jar," he said.

"We were trying to help."

He shrugged. "As a group, you seemed a little bit afraid of us." Their childhoods had unfolded such a short distance from each other, but were radically different.

They rolled through a neighborhood where the large houses were behind gates.

"Are you thinking about how different our childhoods were?"

Did she know him that well already? "You must have grown up around here."

Her voice dropped half an octave, and she stared at her fingers. "Yeah, my old house is about five blocks that way."

"Think you'll ever go back?" He drove past a house with a groomed lawn.

"Not as long as Eric's there." She ran her fingers through her hair. "But he might be leaving."

"So, it's a possibility," he said.

She crossed her arms over her chest. "I don't think I would fit in here anymore. I don't know where I belong."

He felt an empathetic stab to his own gut. His phone buzzed.

She glanced at the phone. "It's Gabriel." Her voice had a hopeful lilt to it. But then she wrinkled her forehead.

"Read the text out loud," he said.

"He says he's been back a few hours, and he's taking inventory in the store."

"That means he's trying to figure out if other agents are involved."

"He wants to meet us at the Woodland Park Zoo in an hour by the lion cages," she said.

He switched lanes of traffic. "Guess we're going to the zoo today. We can kill time there or we can keep driving around."

"Do you think it'll be safe?"

"I don't know." Agent Brown knew he'd got out of jail, but he didn't notice anyone following them. "We can drive around awhile longer."

He switched lanes again as the sign for the zoo came up. Hopefully, Gabriel could arrange some sort of protective custody for Samantha. Once she identified Agent Brown as the man who had tried to kill them, they could get the ball rolling on how deep the corruption went.

He wanted her to be safe more than anything, but he had to admit, he would miss riding around in a car with her and the way her voice reminded him of spring rains and ocean waves.

# FOURTEEN

Samantha's nerves were rattled by the time they got to the security gates at the zoo. The crowds were thick, and every time someone bumped up against her, she was sure her life was over. Yet when she glanced around, she didn't see anyone who looked threatening.

Diego edged in close to her. The drive and parking had consumed some time. They had maybe twenty minutes to spare before they met up with Gabriel. As busy as it was, it would take them ten minutes to get to the lions' cage.

"Do you want some ice cream?" Diego asked.

He must have picked up on her edginess and was trying to calm her with food. They'd known each other such a short time, and yet he seemed tuned in to her emotions.

"Sure," she said. "Strawberry sounds good." She watched the crowd while he stood in line at the ice-cream cart. He glanced back at her several times. Throngs of children pushed in around her.

A Hispanic man with a scar that ran from his mouth to his ear stopped and glared at her. Her skin crawled. She hurried over to where Diego stood in line. When she looked around again, the crowd had swallowed up the man with the scar.

He brushed his fingers lightly over her forearm. "Everything okay?"

"Just expecting the worst," she said.

"No surprise there, given what we have been through so far." He studied the people around them. "With this many people around, we're pretty safe. Plus it would be hard to get a gun past security."

An older woman leaned over the counter. "What do you want, sir?" Diego ordered two ice-cream cones—one chocolate and one strawberry.

He handed the strawberry to her. She licked up the sugary creaminess. They walked past a fountain, and the crowd thinned a little bit. Could they just pretend they were a normal couple out for a day at the zoo?

Diego spoke. "So what did you see that made you so nervous?"

"A guy with a scar on his face, all the way across his cheek to his ear."

Diego stuttered in his step.

Her chest grew tight. "You know who he is?"

"He is a well-known member of the Piru gang. It doesn't mean anything. Not every gang member is out to get us."

"But you said Agent Brown would have known when we got out of the bail hearing. There is a possibility we were followed even if we didn't see anyone," she said.

"Yes, it's possible." Diego's phone buzzed. He glanced down at the text.

"Change of plans. Gabriel's meeting us by the carousel. He says it's busier." Diego placed a protective hand on her back.

She took in a breath and tried not to panic. As he led her through the crowds, she edged closer to him.

The music of the carousel rose above the murmur of

the crowd. Mostly moms with children and some fathers stood watching the colorfully painted horses. There were two men who didn't seem to have kids standing off away from the crowd.

"I don't see Gabriel. Let's circle around." Diego's voice held a little tension. It took a lot to rattle him, but even he must be a little worried that they had walked into a trap.

"There he is." Diego tilted his head toward a tall man with short dark hair walking away from the carousel.

"Where's he going?"

"Maybe he thought it wasn't safe. We'll follow him at a distance. When he feels like we are in the clear, he'll let us know."

She looked back over her shoulder. One of the men who had been standing off by himself was no longer there. She scanned the crowd.

They walked past the Willawong Station with animals from Australia in it.

A man bumped up hard against her.

"'Scuse me," he said to her and then turned and faced the man behind him. "Could you not push me, please?"

The man who had done the pushing was the guy she'd seen earlier who had the scar on his face. His face held a menacing expression. His lip curled back slightly.

Diego pulled her quickly toward a restroom away from the crowd. Trees populated her view on the back side of the small building. She could still hear the murmuring and the footsteps of the crowd, though it dropped in volume.

"I saw Scarface, too," he said. "Best not to take any chances."

"Now we have lost sight of your friend." Her heart pounded against her rib cage.

"We'll find him again or he'll text me." He twisted his body and stared around the side of the building. "I hope."

"Can you see Scarface out there?"

He shook his head and then rested his back against the wall. His hand slipped into hers. The electrified heat of his touch took her by surprise. He'd held her hand before but always it was because they were running. He bent his head toward her so his hair brushed her cheek.

The gesture was more powerful than their kiss earlier. The sweetness of it made her smile.

He made eye contact. "I think we'd be okay to head out now." His voice had a husky quality.

"All right." When she looked up into his eyes, she saw affection there.

If only it could last.

They headed back out into the crowd. They walked past a display called the Bamboo Forest. Monkeys leaped from tree to tree and chattered to the giraffes down below.

Diego took his phone out and read the text. "He's over by the gift shop."

They hurried across the grounds. She watched the crowd, expecting one of the men she'd seen earlier to charge toward them.

They entered the gift shop and found Gabriel at the back of the store behind a stuffed-animal display. Diego and Gabriel greeted each other with a nod.

"Let me do the talking." Gabriel barely glanced at Samantha. "The rumor going around is that you are the one who started working for the other side. My guess is Agent Brown is the one who started that."

"Me?" Diego slammed his palm on his chest. His face

grew red. "That explains the cold reception I got at the field office."

Gabriel held up a hand, indicating Diego needed to be quiet. "Agent Brown is involved and maybe another guy in the same field office. My suspicion is he was getting some sort of kickback for letting this Princeton drug dealer know what the Bureau's next move was."

"How did he find out I was the CI?"

"There is a record of some hacks into reports. We thought they were from outsiders. They might have been from him, manipulating our systems to pose as an outsider." Gabriel took a few steps toward a book display, watching the entrance to the store.

Diego curled his hands into fists but remained quiet so Gabriel could talk. It clearly bothered him to be falsely accused. "He's been able to track us. He must be getting access to incoming messages or something."

"We need to work with a different field office or another agency to get you guys into protective custody." Gabriel looked at Samantha. "Here's what I need you to do. Get to the east parking lot, section E4. I'm in a blue van. I'll wait for you." His gaze went back to the entrance. He jerked nervously as his eyes grew wide. "Back door." He took off.

Gabriel was gone before Diego could respond. By the time they stepped out the back door, he'd vanished. Someone he felt threatened by must have entered the store.

Diego pointed. "Let's blend with those people."

They hurried to integrate into the middle of a crowd that was snaking its way in the general direction of the exit. Samantha glanced over her shoulder, wondering whom Gabriel had seen at the door.

People dispersed, and Diego quickened his pace. The

crowd had taken them the long way toward the exit past the bird-of-prey exhibit. There were hardly any people in this part of the park. Maybe it was a good thing they were completely out in the open. They could see someone coming for them.

They pushed through the exit turnstile. The lot was full of cars but not many people. Most people came in the morning and stayed all day.

She scanned the lot, looking for E4.

"This way." Diego took off at a brisk pace.

She heard the roar of a car engine behind them and turned to see a car zooming at them.

Diego pushed her toward the parked cars. She fell on her knees. Tiny pebbles poked her skin. Diego lifted her to her feet.

Crouching, they wove through the parked cars while their attacker continued to circle the lot. Gabriel's blue van was clearly visible. In order to get to the van, they'd be exposed again on the road.

"Let's go for it," said Diego.

They ran the length of road toward the van. The car appeared at the other end of the lot. The driver increased his speed. Samantha's feet pounded the hard concrete. The roar of the engine grew louder.

The van pulled out of its space and sped toward them.

The car was so loud it felt as if it were on top of them.

The van squealed to a stop. Diego yanked open the door. She jumped in, and he got in behind her. Both of them squeezed in on the single seat. She peered through the windshield. The other car was still coming toward them.

Before Diego had even slammed the door, Gabriel hit the gas and turned the wheel sharply. The other car scraped the driver's-side door, propelled through the parking lot.

Gabriel cranked the wheel and headed toward the exit. "I'm sure he'll get turned around and come after us."

Still breathless from the run, Samantha slipped into the backseat. They drove for some time leaving the city. "Where are we going?"

Gabriel watched the road. "To another FBI field office. They can at least get you into protective custody and take your statement."

"They might want to watch who Agent Brown communicates with in the next twenty-four hours to see how extensive the corruption is, don't you think?" Diego leaned back in the seat. "Once he knows Samantha has made the ID, he's going to be on the run."

"Samantha's ID only lets us charge him with attempted murder—it's not proof of corruption," Gabriel said.

"He came to that island to kill me. He had inside info of which cabin I was in. Surely that's enough to build a case against him that he was dirty," Diego said.

Samantha listened to the banter between the two men, growing very tired. How long had it been since she'd slept more than an hour or so at a time? She laid her head down on the seat while the men continued to rework the plan.

More than anything, she wanted to see to it that Agent Brown went to jail. If he didn't, all of this would be for nothing, and he would still be on the street, waiting to kill her.

Diego looked over his shoulder at Samantha while she slept. Even after being dragged through the mud and water for days, she was beautiful.

Gabriel hit his blinker and took an exit.

"Where are we going?"

"To a friend's cabin. You guys can get cleaned up and

rested while I make some phone calls and see if I can set something up with the office in Everett."

"I don't smell that bad." Diego sniffed his shirt.

Gabriel waved his hand in front of his nose. *"Huele a patas."*

Both men laughed. They'd been friends since they were five years old. The chiding and the humor came naturally. Gabriel headed up a winding dirt road until he came to a cabin.

Gabriel parked the van in the driveway. "I'll go unlock it. You can wake her up."

Diego jumped out of the van and opened the side door. She looked so peaceful sleeping he didn't want to disturb her. Instead, he gathered her in his arms.

Gabriel was waiting by the open door when Diego carried her across the threshold.

"There's a bedroom just off the kitchen." Diego carried Samantha through the rustic cabin and laid her on the bed. He grabbed a throw from a chair and covered her with it. She didn't even stir.

Diego walked back through the kitchen, where Gabriel had tossed bacon into a frying pan and was talking on the phone. From the fragments of conversation Diego caught, Gabriel was talking to another agent.

Gabriel pulled the phone away from his ear. "Chow in a few minutes." The aroma of bacon filled the room. "Should be a towel in that bathroom."

Diego couldn't deny he was eager to take a shower. It felt good to wash the grime off. When he stepped out, he saw that Gabriel had laid pants and a sweatshirt by the door.

After getting dressed, he stepped out into the kitchen,

expecting to see Gabriel. The frying pan was still on. The bacon had turned black.

It felt as if a rock had dropped into his stomach as he hurried over to shut off the gas flame. Eggs, mixed in a bowl and ready to scramble, sat beside the stove.

Gabriel had left quickly or been taken. Shoving down the rising panic, Diego rushed into the bedroom. Samantha still lay curled up asleep. He took a breath and ran back to the living room. The door was slightly ajar but the van was still parked in the driveway. Moving from window to window, he scanned the landscape. The outdoor light didn't provide much illumination, but he didn't see Gabriel anywhere.

He rifled through the kitchen drawers until he found a flashlight. He debated if he should wake Samantha or let her sleep. What if Gabriel had only raced out to deal with some menacing wildlife? Still, in that situation he would have taken the time to turn the burner off. Something more threatening than a bear had shown up. Samantha would be safer if she was awake so she could stay with him.

He hurried to the bedroom and gently shook her shoulder.

Her eyes popped open and she smiled at him. "You smell nice." Her expression became more alarmed when she focused in on the look on his face. "What is it?"

"Gabriel left the cabin in a hurry while I was in the shower. I'm not sure what we're dealing with," he said.

She sat up, still wobbly from sleep. She slipped back into her shoes and followed him through the living room. They stepped out into the crisp night air.

They walked a short distance until the flashlight revealed another car pulled over to the side of the dirt road. It didn't look as if anyone was inside.

"Stand back," he said. He shone the light in the window and then opened the door and peered inside.

Samantha went around to the other side of the car. "The door on this side is open. Like they jumped out quickly and didn't take the time to shut it."

Gabriel must have seen the approaching headlights and run out to intercept them.

A gunshot reverberated from the nearby trees so loud that it felt like a punch to his eardrums. A second shot from a different kind of gun rang out.

"We have to go help him." Diego took off running.

They entered the trees. The scent of cordite was still in the air but the clearing was quiet. He heard no human sounds, only the creaking of the trees.

Samantha caught up with him and stood close. Maybe he should have had her stay behind. No guarantee, though, that whoever was in the car wouldn't just grab her out of the cabin.

She pressed close to him and whispered, "There, I saw something out of the corner of my eye."

It could be a trap. Then again, Gabriel might be lying on the forest floor bleeding to death.

Diego ran out in front. He was tempted to call Gabriel's name but knew that might draw attention.

He heard another gunshot and ran toward the sound. He slowed as he got closer, slipping behind a tree. He grabbed Samantha before she ran ahead.

He pulled her close and whispered in her ear. "There, really close. Listen."

He heard movement—grunting, branches breaking.

The two men were on top of them almost before he could react.

An object hit the side of his head. His world went black. The last thing he heard was Samantha screaming.

# FIFTEEN

Samantha recognized one of the men from the zoo, the man with the scar. He aimed a gun at Diego's head. "We should just shoot him now."

"No," she screamed, trying to twist free of the second man, who gripped her arm. He jerked her back.

Scarface kept the gun aimed at the motionless Diego. Samantha held her breath while her heart raged against her rib cage.

"Brown wants these two dead but he wants to talk to them first," said the second man.

"What about that other guy?" said Scarface.

"Forget about him."

Twenty yards away, a gunshot split through the silence.

"It's that agent coming. We gotta bounce," said Scarface. "Use her as a shield."

Second Man looked down at Diego. "We can't carry him. Come on. Let's just go. At least we'll get paid for her."

They dragged Samantha deeper in the trees. She fought to get away, hitting her kidnapper's meaty arm with her fists.

"Gabriel!" she screamed. The assailant slapped a hand over her mouth.

"Try that again and you'll be dead." The venom in the man's voice told her he was serious. So much for bringing her in alive.

He forced her to go back down the road. One of them opened the car door. The other shoved her in the backseat. Her cheek grazed the rough fabric of the upholstery.

Both men glanced over their shoulders as they jumped into the car. Scarface drove while the other one started talking on the phone to Brown about what had gone wrong. The conversation was a series of yeses and nos and then he hung up.

"What did he say?" said Scarface as he made his way down the road.

"He said not to worry about not getting Cruz. We can use her for bait. Drive slow so they have time to catch up."

Samantha cringed. Would Diego figure out they were setting a trap?

"Gonna take a few minutes for him to wake up from the bash we gave his head and then he'll come for her, huh?"

Second Man shifted in his seat. "Brown says from what he saw on the island, Cruz would die for her."

Her heart melted even more toward Diego. If an enemy could see that level of devotion and desire to protect, it must be true.

Scarface laughed. "It will be what kills him in the end."

His laughter was like a sword cutting through her. She didn't want Diego to die because of her. And she didn't want to die. Not when she was beginning to see how much he cared about her.

"Brown will meet us at the bottom of the hill. He's still

at the all-night diner where we dropped him off. After we are done with our business, he said to pick him up. He wants pics showing we finished what we started."

Evidence of killing them would be on Scarface's phone. So Agent Brown had separated himself from the killing he had planned. Now that he knew the heat was on him, it looked as if Agent Brown was doing everything to keep his hands clean and frame someone else.

Scarface glanced in the rearview mirror. "Looks like they took the bait."

Samantha lifted her head to look out the back window. Her chest tightened at the sight of the glaring headlights.

"Keep your head down," Scarface said. "Don't try to warn them. Or I'll just pop you right now."

She squeezed her eyes shut. Was there anything she could do? There must be some way to warn Diego, to get him to back off. They both didn't have to die.

She lifted her head again. The van barreled toward the back of the car. Samantha swallowed a scream. Diego must be planning to sabotage their car before they got to the base of the hill.

The impact of the van on the back of the car caused her to roll to the floor. The driver cursed. The van bumped a second time. The smaller car swung to one side. The van pushed against the side of the car. Metal crinkled. The two kidnappers shouted expletives as the van plowed the smaller car down the road.

"Get control! Right now—get control," screamed Second Man.

Scarface swiveled the steering wheel. "I'm doing my best." He pressed the gas, causing the engine to varoom.

"He's pushing us toward that tree," said Second Man.

"I can see that," Scarface said through gritted teeth. "Move your head."

When Samantha peered up from the floor, she saw that Scarface had pulled his gun and was aiming toward the van windshield. She swung her leg up and knocked against his hand just as he pulled the trigger. Glass shattered. The shot went wild, but Scarface managed to hold on to the gun.

Scarface turned beet red. He glared down at Samantha, aiming the gun at her head. Her heart squeezed tight as she closed her eyes and prepared to die. She couldn't regret her action, though. Not if it saved Diego.

The car jolted and shook. More metal crunched. The two men shouted as they were jostled around like dried beans in a can. Samantha felt her body being flung from side to side. Her back banged into something. The movement and crunching of metal stopped. She lay stunned and blinking. The roar of the van backing up hit her ears.

The front seat was completely silent. Her door creaked open as she felt Diego's strong arms lifting her and pulling her out. She saw night sky above her. Everything else seemed to be whirling around her. He planted her on her feet, wrapping his arm around her waist to steady her.

The two men in the car had recovered and were banging on the car doors. Diego had plowed the car against a tree and aimed it so one door was blocked by the tree and the other was crushed. The men were trapped.

One of them picked up his gun and aimed it through the window.

She heard glass breaking behind her as Diego helped her to the van, where Gabriel waited behind the wheel. He pushed her in the backseat and got in behind her. Another shot pinged off the side of the van.

Gabriel hit the gas so hard the wheels spun.

"Agent Brown is waiting for them at the bottom of the hill at an all-night café," said Samantha.

"I know which one she's talking about," Gabriel responded.

"I'm sure the men will phone him," she said. "It doesn't sound like he has a car."

"That's probably not a problem for Agent Brown. I'm sure he'll just *acquire* one."

"We can't drive faster than a phone call." Gabriel stared out at the dark road ahead.

"He'll probably be looking for us to come down the hill." Fear twisted around her throat and settled in her belly. "But he didn't want to come up the hill after us himself and get his hands dirty. What do you suppose he'll do?"

Diego shook his head. "I think he's pretty desperate. His life is over once we make the case against him."

"Those guys back there said he wanted to talk to us before he killed us. He probably wants to find out how much we know," she said.

"Let's head to Everett. I'll see if we can have an agent meet us somewhere instead of waiting until the field office opens," Gabriel said. "Soon as we are past the café, you can take over driving, Diego, so I can make calls."

They made it to the bottom of the hill. She saw the café right away. As they sped past, she noticed two different cars pulling out onto the road.

She peered out the back window and wondered if one of those cars held Agent Brown.

Without stopping the car, Diego and Gabriel switched places. Diego noticed Samantha's stunned look in the rearview mirror.

Gabriel slipped into the backseat beside her and elbowed her. "It's a trick we used to do in high school. Why don't you sit up front with Diego while I make this phone call."

Samantha slipped into the front passenger seat and offered Diego a shy smile. The look in her eyes electrified the space between them.

She touched her hair. "I must look pretty bad. At least you got a shower."

"You look fine, just fine." He thought she was beautiful, actually. But the last time he'd pointed that out, it had backfired. Something seemed to have shifted between them. They were growing closer, but both of them knew there was a time approaching when they wouldn't have a reason to stay together.

The road started showing signs for Everett and then the lights of the city came into view. He'd lost track of the two cars that had pulled out of the café parking lot behind them. He clenched his teeth. He preferred having his enemies where he could see them. Brown wouldn't give up easily; he knew that much.

Gabriel spoke in a low voice, but it didn't sound as if he was making much progress connecting them with an agent. The sun came up as they entered the city. Finally, he pulled his phone away from his ear. "Agents can meet us at the field office in three hours. They will take you to a safe house. I'll stay with you through the handoff and then I've gotta get back to work."

"Three hours. Why so long?" Diego studied the exit signs.

"It's Sunday. Everybody thinks they should have the day off. These guys like to pretend they have a nine to five, but they are supposed to be available round the clock."

"That gives us time to get some food," Diego said.

"I'd really like to shower," said Samantha.

Diego drove around until he found a motel. The place looked a little run-down, but it would do for three hours.

"I'll go get food," said Gabriel. "You can keep watch."

Diego and Samantha got out of the van.

"I'll text the room number to you," Diego said.

Gabriel nodded and then drove off. They caught the motel clerk sleeping in a chair. The old woman jerked awake when Diego rang the bell on the counter.

"So sorry, don't get many people coming in at this hour." Her gaze held a hint of suspicion as she narrowed her eyes at them. "Check-in isn't really until later today."

He threw a twenty on the counter. "I can pay extra for the early check-in."

"Room 19." The clerk handed the key to Samantha.

They stepped outside. Diego remained on high alert as they walked across the lot to their room.

He stuck the key in the motel-room door, pushed the door open and let her step past him. He scanned the parking lot, making a mental note of each car, not seeing any sign of Agent Brown or anyone suspicious. And even that made him nervous. Maybe Brown was trying to rustle up some more muscle to do his dirty work. All the same, Diego was pretty sure someone had followed them into the city. It was just a matter of time before the corrupt agent or his associates made a move.

Diego texted the room number to Gabriel, then placed his phone on the night table by the bed. He focused his attention on the parking lot while standing to the side of the window so he wouldn't be seen. He heard the shower running in the bathroom.

Twenty minutes passed and Samantha came out of the bathroom looking refreshed. She combed her fingers through her hair. "Wish I had some clean clothes." She sat down in the only chair in the room. "Where's Gabriel?"

Diego picked up his phone and checked the time. "I'm not sure. Maybe he drove back to Seattle to get the food." He tried to sound lighthearted, but a knot of tension formed in his stomach. They'd passed food trucks that were less than five minutes away.

The smile fell from her face, as well. "Maybe you should call him."

He picked up the phone and dialed his friend's number. The phone rang five times and then went to message.

"He might be driving and can't pick up." She sounded as if she was trying to convince herself.

Samantha turned on the television and clicked through channels. She dropped the remote twice and kept sending Diego nervous glances. Another ten minutes went by. Diego stared out at the parking lot, growing more tense with each passing minute.

Samantha clicked off the TV and paced the floor.

Diego jumped when his phone rang. It was Gabriel's number.

He let out the breath he'd been holding in. "Hey, what's taking you so long?"

His question was answered with an extended silence as the tension returned to Diego's muscles. "Gabriel?" He glanced up at Samantha, who stood as still as a statue.

"He wants you to come to the boat graveyard at the

first pullout." Gabriel kept his voice steady but Diego heard the fear behind each word.

Diego slumped down on the bed. "Does he want to trade you for us?"

"Yes. If you are not here in fifteen minutes, he shoots me."

Agent Brown wanted to ensure they didn't have time to go for help. "We don't have a car."

"It's not more than a five-minute taxi ride. It's out by the Sound near Steamboat Slough... Hurry."

"We'll be there," he said. His throat went tight with emotion. "Gabriel, I've always loved you like a brother."

"I know, *cuate.* It seems like an elusive dream now that you and I could be brothers."

Diego tilted his head sideways. Elusive dream? Gabriel didn't talk like that. His friend was trying to tell him something. "We'll get there as fast as we can." And he meant it. His friend was not going to die because of him.

They took off jogging at a steady pace, crossing several busy streets until they saw a taxi. Diego's heart was pounding by the time they got into the car.

"The boat graveyard, and please hurry," said Diego.

The taxi driver nodded. "I can get you there in five."

They zigzagged through the city until the Sound came into view. The taxi driver let them off at a pullout where they had a clear view of all the out-of-commission boats, some half out of the water, some only partially visible, all of them rotting and weathered.

Diego studied the boats. The river stretched for some distance. He pulled Samantha back toward some trees. "Wait. How much time do we have?"

Samantha glanced at her watch. "We've used up seven minutes."

"Gabriel was trying to tell me something. He used the phrase *elusive dream*. He doesn't talk like that." Diego's mind raced. Maybe it was the name of a boat he was on. He peered over his shoulder, looking out at the string of defunct boats. "We've got eight minutes. Let's see if we can get the jump on him. The way Agent Brown set it up, he wants to see us coming. Maybe just to pick us off."

"You mean he never intended to let Gabriel go," Samantha said. "Maybe he gave up on talking to us first."

"Brown doesn't want witnesses, remember? If he can get info from us, he will, but the bottom line is he wants us dead." They moved along the trees and bushes. Diego surveyed the boats. Gabriel must be in a place where he could see the name *Elusive Dream* but Agent Brown could not, otherwise he wouldn't have used that kind of code.

"There." Samantha pointed across the river at a boat with its hull stuck in the water. "*Elusive Dream*, but how did they get across?"

Diego peered through the bushes. "They didn't. Gabriel's in that boat on this side of the river, but he's positioned where he can see out across the water. Come on. We've got to hurry." If Gabriel wasn't already dead…

*Please, God, no, not my friend.*

The assumption Diego was operating on was that Brown expected them to come right out in the open from the pullout where they'd been told to go. That meant that he must be in some high spot, waiting to put a bullet in both of them. Brown had already demonstrated back at the island that he had sniper skills.

They ran toward the boat. It creaked and groaned as the water beat against it. The boat looked as though it would fall apart if they stepped on it. They scrambled up the ladder. Diego turned a half circle. He saw Agent Brown jumping from one boat to the next on his way toward them, then crouching low to hide when he realized he'd been spotted.

Samantha jerked when she saw him. "We don't have much time before he gets here."

"You stay topside. Go to the shore. There is no reason for both of us to be trapped."

She hesitated for only a second. She was smart enough to see the logic of the plan. Chances were Diego and Gabriel would not make it, but he had to try.

Diego stepped down the ladder into the ship's cabin. Gabriel was tied to a post facing the window that looked out on *Elusive Dream*. Diego pulled his pocketknife and cut the rope that bound Gabriel. Agent Brown's thudding footfall sounded above them. He was on the boat.

"Through the window," said Diego.

Gabriel crawled through. Diego heard him splash into the water. A shot was fired down into the hull as Diego pushed his head through the window and dived into the cool, murky water.

His last thought was that at least he had managed to save Samantha if not himself and his friend.

# SIXTEEN

From the bushes where she hid, Samantha winced with each gunshot that was fired. She caught the muffled sound of water splashing. On the boat deck, Agent Brown held his gun up but didn't take aim. Her heart leaped. Maybe Diego and Gabriel had made it out. She moved farther downriver, careful to shield herself from view by hiding behind the boat rubble, scrap metal and bushes that grew along the shore.

Agent Brown gave up searching the water and jumped off the boat. She saw Gabriel's head rise to the surface as he took a breath before disappearing again. Her heart squeezed tight. Where was Diego? She wasn't going to give up hope, not yet. At least Gabriel had made it out.

She rushed ahead, diving behind a chunk of twisted metal. Her foot hit something, and one piece of metal pinged against another. She cringed, pressing lower to the ground. Agent Brown's footfall slowed and then stopped altogether.

She sucked in a breath, trying not to move at all. If he found her, there was no place to run. She'd be dead in seconds.

She heard a single footstep on the hard ground.

*Please, God, no, I don't want to die.*

The metal above her creaked from a gust of wind.

*Let him think it was the wind the time before.*

She waited, counting the seconds, listening. Silence. He wasn't moving at all. Her heartbeat drummed in her ears so loudly, she was afraid it would give her away. Her leg cramped and strained from the strange position she'd crouched in.

She hadn't heard Agent Brown walk away. He was still out there…close and watching. She could almost feel him breathing down her neck.

Why wasn't he moving?

How much longer was this going to go on? She really needed to shift to ease the discomfort in her leg.

Then she heard it, rapid footsteps moving toward her. Agent Brown loomed over her, his gun pointed at her face. Instinctively her hands went up to her head, and she looked away from her assassin. A thudding noise pounded her eardrums.

When she looked up, Diego had taken Agent Brown to the ground.

She couldn't leave him. This was her battle, too.

Diego's wet clothes weighed him down and made him move slower as they slapped against his body. Agent Brown swung a leg out and caught Diego on the back of the knees. He buckled to the ground and then the agent was on top of him. Downriver, Gabriel crawled out of the water and lumbered toward the fight. Agent Brown's gun had gone flying toward the bushes when Diego hit him from behind. She didn't see it anywhere. She didn't know how to use one anyway. Gabriel would not get here fast enough.

Agent Brown wrestled Diego until he was on top of

him. He fastened his hands around Diego's neck and squeezed.

Diego wasn't going to die, not today, not any day. Not if she could prevent it. Samantha picked up a piece of old wood and swung it at Agent Brown's back. He arched his back, and his hands flew up. The wood split in two.

Diego yanked on Agent Brown's collar, drawing him closer and then punching him in the jaw. The blow stunned him but he remained on top of Diego. Brown's face turned crimson and murder filled his eyes. He reached again for Diego's neck.

"Get off him." Samantha lunged at the agent, pushing him with the full force of her weight.

He looked to the side, jumped to his feet and scrambled across the sand. He reached into some brush and pulled out his gun.

Gabriel came up behind Diego and Samantha.

Brown lifted the gun and aimed it at Samantha. Diego slipped in front of her. "You can't take out all three of us."

The laughter and banter of people filled the air. Four people carrying kayaks appeared through the trees.

Agent Brown placed his gun out of view behind his back. "This is not over." He turned and disappeared into the trees.

"He'll follow us. You know he will," said Gabriel.

"Let's get to the field office," Diego said.

"I don't have the van anymore. He took the keys."

Fear coiled inside Samantha's stomach. That meant time spent dodging Agent Brown without the protection that the van afforded them.

"We'll take a taxi to the field office and wait around there even if the office is locked," Diego said.

"No, I think it's safer to show up right when the agents

get there. Waiting around makes us an easy target. We stay on the move, and we work our way toward the office."

Diego nodded in understanding. "We won't give away that that is where we're going until the last minute."

Samantha stared at the trees, and her chest tightened. "He's probably watching us now. What if he heard our plan?"

The four people with their kayaks stared at the three of them. They must look quite a sight, Gabriel and Diego both soaking wet, Samantha in dirty clothes that she'd been wearing for far too long.

One member of the kayaking party came toward them. "Are you guys all right?"

"We're fine," said Diego.

"You look like you could use a towel at least." The man pointed through the trees. "We left some out on the dock. Feel free."

She liked that the man offered kindness and help without questions. He could see that they were in need, but didn't press for explanations. It was a story they couldn't begin to tell.

She could feel Agent Brown watching them as they made their way to the dock to get dried off. A few cars whizzed by on the road, but they saw no sign of a taxi. Most of the land around them was forest and there were no other people. She could hear the sound of trains in the distance, but there were no other hints of traffic.

"We need to get to where there are more people," Diego said.

Gabriel glanced around. "Let's put some distance between us and Agent Brown. He'll need time to run back to his car if that is how he's going to play it."

"Let's run where he can't drive." Diego pointed off

toward the sound of the train yard. They ran through a strip of trees and crossed a road before the clacking of trains on rails became more distinct.

When Samantha glanced over her shoulder, she saw a car moving slowly along the road. Probably Agent Brown tracking where they were going.

They entered the train yard, crossing tracks and stopping to wait for trains to pass. The clamor of the moving trains, along with bells and whistles, drowned out all other sound. They came to a set of tracks that was under repair where the noise was not quite as oppressive.

All three of them stopped to catch their breath.

Even though Diego leaned close to Gabriel, he had to shout to be heard. "Can you call your friend in the Bureau? Let them know the situation. See if they can pick us up."

Gabriel nodded. "When we get to where we can be heard."

They ran through the edge of the train yard and out onto an industrial street occupied by warehouses and factories. Samantha glanced over her shoulder. It looked as if they'd eluded Agent Brown...for now.

Diego ran so hard it felt as if his lungs had been scraped with a knife. His leg muscles screamed from the strain of their all-out sprint. As they made their way through the warehouse district, a sense of relief filled him. Agent Brown might have seen which way they'd gone but he hadn't been able to follow. They would have seen him.

They walked past a multistory metal building surrounded by two cranes. Where were they, anyway? He checked his GPS. His cheap phone wasn't working. It had got too wet. "We need to figure out how to get to the field office."

They walked until the industrial buildings gave way to tire stores and car lots, many of them closed because it was Sunday. He didn't see a coffee shop or any place where they could get directions.

Gabriel hit Diego's shoulder with his fist. "That car showroom is open."

Diego stared down at his muddy clothes. And then at the showroom filled with high-end cars. They'd dried off some in their run, but he still looked like a homeless man. "They'll take one look at us and then kick us out."

"All we need is someone to point us in the right direction," said Gabriel.

Diego threw up his hands. "What about them coming to get us?"

"We still need to figure out where we're at first," said Gabriel.

The noise of the city street was cut off as they stepped through the glass door. Easy-listening music played at a low volume. The showroom floor featured red and yellow sports cars. In a glass office on the other side of the showroom, a man talking on the phone spotted them. Hopefully, his phone conversation would take only a few minutes. The man's jaw dropped open when he saw the three of them.

Diego tensed. "Come on, Gabriel. That guy is not going to help us."

Gabriel shook his head as he touched the phone screen. "Mine is blitzing out, too. The water must have ruined it. The GPS isn't working—it can't tell me where we are. We need directions. We've got to at least ask. Maybe he'll give us directions just to get rid of us faster."

The salesman hung up the phone and bolted toward them with a big, insincere grin on his face. "Can I help you folks?"

"Can you point us toward downtown? Rucker Avenue." Gabriel tugged on his muddy sleeve.

The salesman studied them for a long suspicion-filled moment. He pointed through the window. "About twenty blocks due east."

They stepped outside.

"That's a long way to walk." Samantha stared up the street.

He saw no sign of a taxi anywhere. Being out in the open like this was not good. Even if they had shaken Agent Brown, he knew the general direction they'd gone. There weren't that many exits out of the train yard.

A police car roared up behind them. No siren, but its lights were flashing.

Oh, great, the salesman had phoned them in.

The police officer got out of his car. "How are you folks doing today?"

Gabriel's shoulders stiffened. "We haven't broken any laws."

Diego signaled his friend to back down by squeezing his arm above the shoulder. Maybe this was a blessing in disguise.

"If we're making people uncomfortable around here, maybe you could give us a ride," Diego said.

The officer eyeballed them for a moment. "I'm headed downtown to the station. I can take you there."

"Is that anywhere near Rucker Avenue?" Gabriel had caught on to his plan.

The officer narrowed his eyes at them, probably trying to figure out what their game was. "It's in the same part of town."

"Take us there, then." Diego tilted his head toward the auto dealers. "We don't want to make anyone uneasy."

The officer nodded. "Get in."

Once they were all in the car, the police officer radioed in what he was doing. The drive across town took only a few minutes. The officer let them out on a crowded street outside the police station.

Diego leaned close to the police officer. "Can you point us in the direction of Rucker Avenue?"

"Five blocks over that way," said the officer.

Gabriel leaned close to Samantha and Diego. "It's a tall brick building."

People swarmed around them and bumped up against them as they made their way up the street. Samantha walked up ahead of Diego. The sun shone on her honey-colored hair. She was swallowed up by the crowd. He quickened his pace to catch up with her. When he looked at all the heads bobbing in front of him, he didn't see her. Gabriel was several feet behind him.

Fingers wrapped around his wrist and pulled him away from the crowd into a bookshop. Samantha held on to his hand.

Fear danced in Samantha's eyes. "I saw him."

"That's not possible. How could he have followed us?"

"I don't know. I just know it was him across the street outside the police station." Her voice faltered. "He saw me."

Her terror was very real, but he didn't see how Agent Brown could have found them. They'd lost him in the train yard. If Agent Brown had wagered they were headed toward the field office, why not just wait to ambush them there? Why come to the police station? He suspected that fatigue and all they had been through had made her see something that wasn't there. Now was not the time to question her.

"Let's just get to that office." He scanned the bookstore, which had only a few patrons. He addressed his question to the female clerk who bent over the counter reading a very old-looking book. "Is there a back way out of here?"

The clerk pointed without looking up from her book.

Diego craned his neck toward the entrance and the busy street outside. They'd lost Gabriel. Hopefully, he would catch up with them at the field office. Diego held the back door for Samantha. She slipped by him, and they stepped out into an alley. Both the cross streets hummed with activity but the alley was empty.

She tilted her head. "Which way?"

"I'm not sure. Gabriel said it was a tall brick building."

"I'll check down this street. You check that way," she said.

He watched Samantha for a moment as she wandered through the alley. Her long hair looked almost golden in this light. He sprinted up the alley and peered up. The tall brick building Gabriel had described stood out from the others. When he turned back toward the alley, he didn't see Samantha. He ran to the other end of the alley into the bustling street. Still no Samantha. His heart beat a little faster as he studied the faces around him. He swallowed hard to quell the rising panic.

Why hadn't he believed her? Somehow Agent Brown had found them and now he'd taken Samantha.

# SEVENTEEN

Samantha winced at the now familiar sensation of the metal gun barrel poking her spine.

"Just keep moving." Agent Brown's voice was filled with venom.

The crowd whirled around her. If she cried out for help, would he shoot her in public? In the chaos that followed her falling to the ground, he might be able to slip away. She couldn't risk it. He'd escape and she'd be dead.

"How did you find us? I thought we shook you in the train yard."

"I have a police scanner. When that cop picked you up, he called it in. Two men, one woman—the men wet and muddy."

He pushed the gun deeper into her back. Agent Brown stopped, tilting his head. Samantha looked up, as well. The building next to them looked as if it had a floor that was under construction.

"Go into that building and up the stairs."

He must be looking for a place to kill her where there were no people. If he succeeded, it would be over for her. Her mind raced. She had to do something.

She turned suddenly and faced Agent Brown.

"Stop it," she screamed and pushed him on his shoulders. "How dare you touch me there."

A stunned looked flashed across Agent Brown's face. He shoved his gun in his waistband to hide it as several people stopped and looked at them.

Agent Brown shook his head. "What are you talking about?"

"The cop station is just around the corner, buddy. I could have you arrested." She injected as much righteous indignation as she could muster.

Agent Brown's face turned red. "You're lying."

Several people continued to observe the fight on the street.

She pointed at him. "You'd better keep your hands off women you don't know." Lifting her chin, she whirled around and stalked away, increasing her pace. She needed to get away. He would make a rush for her as soon as the attention was no longer on him.

She hurried up the block. She breathed a sigh of relief when Diego appeared, running toward her through the crowd.

"He's behind us," she said.

They quickened their pace. "I'm sorry I didn't believe you."

She glanced over her shoulder but didn't see their pursuer. She surveyed the side streets. No doubt he had some trick up his sleeve.

Diego pointed toward the tall brick building. They sprinted up the sidewalk where the crowds were much thinner. By the time they stepped into the lobby, they were both out of breath.

"Why do you suppose he didn't follow us?"

"If he shows his face in this building, the agents could take him in once we point him out," Diego said.

Samantha wanted to believe they were finally safe. "I hope Gabriel made it. We don't have a lot of clout without him."

"I hope the rumors Agent Brown spread about me haven't reached this far." He walked over to a wall and studied the directory. "They're on the fourth floor."

As they stepped into the elevator, she could feel the tension coiling around her torso. Agent Brown wouldn't give up easily. They couldn't let their guard down until they were at that safe house.

She reached for Diego's hand and gave it a little squeeze.

"Almost safe," he said.

She watched the numbers on the elevator tick by. With each passing floor, the tension fell away.

"That was brilliant, by the way, back there on the street—calling Agent Brown out like that so you could get away."

"Thank you," she said.

"You may have missed your calling."

"You mean you can make a living falsely accusing men of harassment?"

He laughed. "No, I just meant you keep your head in dangerous situations. You could do what I do. Or what the agents do."

She loved the admiration she detected in his voice, but knew she couldn't have her nerves hammered to pieces on a regular basis. "I don't know about that, but thanks." Then she wondered if Diego was trying to picture a life where they could be together.

The doors swung open. She half expected Agent Brown

to be standing there with a gun aimed at them. Instead, she had a clear view of the watercooler. The stiffness through her shoulders subsided.

Diego placed his palm lightly on her back. "I know. I was expecting to see him there, too."

She was amazed at how tuned in to her thoughts and feelings he was. Had the trauma and the danger bonded them or was it something deeper, an affection and understanding that would survive after this was all over? Hard to say.

They stepped out into a hallway that had a series of closed doors, but no reception area.

He knocked on the first door. A man opened it and looked at them from head to toe.

"Diego Cruz and his witness," said the man.

Diego nodded. "Has Gabriel Tovar shown up?"

The man stepped outside his office. "This way." The agent made his way down the hall and pushed open a door where Gabriel and another man waited at a table.

Gabriel's face lit up, and he ran and hugged his friend, slapping him loudly on the back. "I lost you in the shuffle."

"I always come through. You know that, bro."

Gabriel gestured toward the other man. "This is Agent Klark."

Agent Klark nodded at both of them. "We need the two of you to make your statements separately."

Gabriel cupped both of Diego's shoulders. "This is the end of the line for me. I do have a real job I need to get back to. One of the agents is giving me a ride back to Seattle. I'm going to be probing around that office but keeping it under the radar."

Diego placed a hand over Gabriel's. "Thanks for everything, brother." Then he pulled his friend into another hug.

Gabriel pulled free of the hug and looked at Samantha. "Take care of him."

Her throat went tight. His words, though spoken softly, had the force of emotion behind them. She nodded. "I'll do my best."

Gabriel must have recognized the growing affection between them. Gabriel left the room and headed down the hallway.

Agent Klark tugged on his tie. "Mr. Cruz, you stay in this room. Miss… What is your last name?"

"James, Samantha James."

"Two doors down, there is a waiting room of sorts."

Samantha offered Diego a quick glance. She knew she was safe now, but something about being away from him made her uneasy. "Okay."

She stepped back out into the hallway. A female agent came toward her holding a stack of folded clothes that she handed to Samantha. "Gabriel said you were in need of some fresh clothes, and we appear to be around the same size. They're what I wear when I have to testify in court. You'll look like you're ready for a business meeting, but they are clean."

"Thank you. Where can I change?"

"The bathroom is at the end of the hall." The agent held out her hand. "I'm Agent Blakely, by the way. You can call me Pam."

Samantha shook Pam's hand and then hurried down the hall. She slipped into a bathroom stall. Even though the clothes, a button-down shirt and dress slacks, were a little stiff, it felt good to get out of the dirty clothes she'd been wearing. She threw the pink shirt and jeans in the trash and stopped for a moment to catch a glimpse of herself in the mirror. She'd have to ask the female agent if she could borrow a comb. She leaned over and splashed water on her face. When she raised her head, Agent Brown was standing behind her in the mirror dressed in a janitor's uniform.

He grinned at her. "You didn't think I'd give up that easy, did you? Couldn't figure out why you left Seattle until I saw you headed this way."

She opened her mouth to scream. He jumped toward her, slapping a hand over her mouth.

"You try it. Just try it." The gun barrel pressed in her side.

She inhaled his rotten egg–smelling breath.

"Now we're going to get out of here real fast. Move toward the stairwell, not the elevator."

She nodded her head. Her whole body trembled with fear as she tried to collect her thoughts. Would he just shoot her in the stairwell? Probably, if there were no people.

They moved out into the empty hallway. He pushed her toward the exit door. He used one hand to cover her mouth and the other to poke the gun in her side. Voices from behind a closed office door grew louder.

Agent Brown's attention was momentarily drawn away from her. The pressure of the gun in her side lightened up a little. She took advantage of the moment, reached back and grabbed the gun thinking she would turn it on him. She didn't know how to use a gun, but Agent Brown didn't know that.

When she grabbed the gun, it went flying, hitting the side of a metal trash can. Agent Brown grabbed her again, twisting her arm behind her at a painful angle.

He inched toward where the gun had fallen. The voices on the other side of the door grew louder. The door clicked open.

Agent Brown dragged her toward the exit door. She caught a glimpse of one of the agents stepping out into the hallway just as the door sealed shut.

Diego watched while Agent Klark typed on his computer, the tapping of the keys the only sound in the room.

"Almost done here," said Agent Klark.

He heard a noise, a sort of tinny sound like metal hitting metal. Without knowing why, the noise caused his heart to beat faster. Diego pushed his chair back from the table. "Can you give me a minute? I want to go check on Samantha."

"Sure."

The noise was probably just the other agent dropping something. All the same, he felt an urgency to make sure Samantha was doing okay. He pushed open the door to the room where she was supposed to be waiting, finding only a sofa and a table piled with magazines.

He hurried down the hall where two of the other agents were talking.

"I can't find Samantha." His voice remained steady despite the thunderstorm brewing in his mind.

The female agent pushed her glasses back on her face. "She stepped into the bathroom to change, but she should be done by now."

Agent Klark came out of the conference room. "Everything okay?"

Diego looked at him. "Samantha is gone. Is there anywhere else she could go in this office?"

Agent Klark shook his head. "It's a small office." He

turned to face the female agent. "Agent Blakely, did you notice anything?"

Agent Blakely shook her head. "I went back to the office after I spoke to her. I'll go check the bathroom."

"She wouldn't leave here by herself, not unless she had to. She's smart. She wouldn't put herself in danger by going back out there alone." Danger must have come to her.

The female agent emerged from the bathroom shaking her head. "There's just a janitor's bucket in there."

Diego scanned the hallway and the closed doors, and then he saw the gun by the trash can. He ran over and picked it up.

"He's got her. Brown must have taken her." Diego's hands tightened into fists. "Is there a back way out of here?"

"Down the stairs and through the parking garage." The female agent hurried back to her office and emerged a second later, snapping her holster around her waist. "We'll go with you."

He only hoped they weren't too late.

Agent Brown had forced her down one flight of stairs when she heard a door open and voices above them. They were coming for her.

After he heard the people coming down the stairs, Agent Brown dragged her out of the stairwell and onto another floor. Some people were in the hall. She caught a glimpse of a florist shop across the hall before he shoved her into a room. She heard the door click shut behind her.

They were in some sort of storage room with shelves of boxes filled with office supplies. He took his hand off her mouth. She screamed and ran back toward the door.

He grabbed her from behind and pulled her back, pushing her against a wall. She reached out for the shelving as she fell backward, and it shook. Her spine impacted with the wall and she slid to the floor, stunned. The shelving continued to sway and vibrate.

Agent Brown pushed a heavy desk in front of the door. He stalked toward her.

Still stunned from her fall, she braced herself by placing her palm on the floor. "They'll know it was you who killed me."

His lip curled back. "I have connections. I'll be out of the country by then."

Why didn't he just get on a plane right away? Why stay around to kill them? Still wobbly, she pushed herself to her feet. He lunged toward her. She darted away, slipping behind the high shelving. He raced around and grabbed her again. This time he wrapped his hands around her neck and squeezed. He sneered. She reached up to his ear and twisted it. He yowled and let go of her.

She ran past two rows of metal shelving and slipped behind the shelf that was close to the wall. Agent Brown was bulkier than she was. He wouldn't be able to get behind there easily.

"You can't hide from me," he said. He yanked the boxes of stuff off the middle shelf and reached for her. She slipped toward the corner of the room. He pulled another box off and threw it on the floor. Now she was trapped. She looked up. Maybe not. With all her strength, she pushed on the shelf. It toppled over, burying Agent Brown in boxes.

She raced toward the door and pushed on the desk. Agent Brown struggled to get out from underneath the shelving and boxes.

The desk was too heavy. She had only seconds to escape. She ran toward the far end of the room, flung open a window and climbed out.

She dropped to the ground and took off running, knowing that Agent Brown would be only seconds behind her.

# EIGHTEEN

Diego and the other two agents raced down the stairs and out into the parking garage. Diego's chest felt as if there were an elephant sitting on it. He couldn't get a deep breath.

He scanned the parking garage, looking for signs of movement. Agent Brown hadn't parked here. His car was probably closer to the police station. Would he steal a car or try to get back to his?

The squeal of tires answered Diego's question. "This way," said Agent Blakely. They ran toward a car. Agent Klark hit the unlock button and got behind the steering wheel. Diego dived into the backseat. Agent Klark backed the car out of the parking space. Agent Blakely grabbed the passenger's-side door and hopped in.

He could see the car leaving the parking garage. "There, he turned left. The red sports car."

Either Agent Brown wasn't thinking clearly or he had grabbed the first car he found unlocked and could hot-wire. A red sports car was easy enough to track…or maybe it wasn't Agent Brown at all?

"Let me out. I'm staying behind," Diego said.

"But…" Agent Klark protested even as he slowed the car.

"We've got to cover all our bases," Diego said. "I don't have a phone."

Agent Blakely tossed him her phone. "We'll call you."

He jumped out of the car before it came to a complete stop, doing a half roll to minimize impact. After searching the parking garage, Diego ran around to the entrance of the building. Samantha had been able to get away from Agent Brown before in a crowd by making a scene. Wouldn't he be reluctant to take her out into a crowd again?

He studied the map of the building on the first floor.

The phone Agent Blakely had given him rang.

"Yes," he said.

"You were right," Agent Blakely said. "A fifty-year-old man was driving the car. We're coming back in."

"In this building, is there any vacant office space where he could take her?" His biggest fear was that Brown had found a private place to kill her and now was just waiting for the chance to leave unnoticed.

"Three floors below us, there's an empty office for lease."

"Can you involve the local police in a search for her without giving details? He couldn't have got far on foot," Diego said.

"We can do that," said Agent Blakely. "Klark is going to come back in and help search the building. I'll coordinate things with the locals."

He hung up and headed toward the empty office on the second floor. The door was locked. The florist shop next door had a Closed sign on the door, but a man was inside painting one of the walls. The counter and shelves were covered in plastic.

"I don't suppose you saw a man with a buzz cut and a blonde woman go by here? The man was probably walking very close to the woman, and she may have seemed distressed."

The painter shook his head.

Maybe Brown had chanced it and tried to make it back to his car. How was he controlling Samantha without a gun? The florist-shop window provided a view of what looked like a newly constructed but unoccupied building.

A flash of movement caught his eye. Samantha appeared running toward the building. Brown was right behind her. Diego raced out of the florist shop and toward the outside door. Knowing that he had only seconds, there was no time to call for backup.

Samantha was only twenty feet from the new glass-walled building when she realized it was still under construction. It looked finished from the outside, but the piles of construction materials suggested it would be empty. When she glanced over her shoulder, Agent Brown was only fifty feet behind her. She dashed inside, hoping to find someone to help her—or at least to deter Brown from attacking her. The first floor was a mostly completed lobby. No one was there.

She didn't see an obvious exit. She ran up the stairs several flights until she found a place to hide. She dived behind a stack of plywood, covering herself with a sheet of plastic she grabbed close by. Only seconds passed before she heard footsteps pounding the floor.

She peered out from beneath the plastic. A tool belt was within her reach. The footsteps grew more distinct. He was searching the other side of the open floor. She stretched her arm and slipped the hammer out of the tool belt.

Agent Brown's footsteps pounded on the flimsy floor,

making it shake. The vibrations told her he was close. She peered out from beneath the plastic to a view of his shoes pointed right at her. Would he think to tear the plastic off or just head up the next floor?

Her heartbeat drummed in her ears.

The plastic crinkled as he reached for it. She swung the hammer hard at his calf and then pounded his toe. Agent Brown groaned in pain and hopped backward.

She burst out from beneath the plastic and ran toward the stairway. Agent Brown was doubled over, gripping his leg. He limped toward her, picking up speed when she tried to escape before jumping at her to tackle her. The weight of his body took her down.

He pulled her hair and yanked the hammer out of her hand. "Get up." He got off her and stood with the hammer ready to hit her.

"They'll catch you."

"Not if it looks like an accident." He tilted his head toward the incomplete outside wall. "Walk toward that scaffolding."

The fire in his eyes told her he would hit her if she didn't. She backed up, keeping her eyes on Agent Brown and then glancing behind her. Could she make a run for it?

He continued to favor the foot she had injured as she drew closer to the open side of the building. The cool air hit her when she neared the edge of the floor. She tried to come up with a way to get to the stairs before he could grab her. She stepped out on the scaffolding. He swung the hammer at her. She dodged the blow. And then another. The third time, he managed to hit her in the shoulder. Pain radiated down her arm.

The scaffolding swayed and banged against the side

of the building as they moved back and forth on it. His eyes were filled with rage as he stalked toward her.

She tried to dash out of his way, but his hand latched on to her shoulder. He backed her up against the scaffold railing and she bent over backward. He dropped the hammer to get a better grip on her. Her feet lifted off the ground. She lost a sense of which way was up as the sky spun around her.

Her hands reached out for the support of the railing, but all she felt was air as she flailed around and Agent Brown pushed her closer to death.

Diego bolted up the stairs to the fourth floor of the half-constructed building. He saw the hammer on the floor and then Agent Brown trying to push Samantha off the scaffolding.

He sprinted to them, slammed his hands on Agent Brown's shoulder and threw him toward the other end of the scaffold. Agent Brown lunged at them, pushing them both against the railing. The scaffolding creaked from their weight.

Agent Brown shoved his forearm under Diego's chin and pushed upward. Diego's back pressed against Samantha as she was squished between him and the railing.

She whispered one word. "Space."

He knew what she meant. He pushed against the pressure Agent Brown applied, so he wasn't pressed so hard against her. She squeezed out from behind him and punched Agent Brown in the stomach. The blow wasn't strong enough to make him let go of Diego, but it was enough so he staggered a bit. Diego took advantage of the distraction. He pushed Agent Brown against the opposite railing, and the agent fell back.

Diego had no intention of running. They'd done enough of that. He wanted this to be over, to have Agent Brown in custody. Right now, the man was unarmed, and he didn't seem to have any of his thugs with him. This may be the best chance Diego was going to get.

Agent Brown barreled toward him, knocking him to the floor of the scaffolding. Samantha grabbed the back of Agent Brown's collar and yanked.

Brown swung around and pushed Samantha through the metal bars that braced the scaffold. Samantha fell, clinging to the metal bars, her body swinging. She reached toward the scaffolding ladder. If she lost her grip, she'd fall a long way.

Agent Brown slipped through the metal bars and crawled down toward Samantha. Diego climbed out onto the lattice-work of the scaffold, seeking to get in between them. He was one length above them as Agent Brown reached out and grabbed for Samantha, gaining a hold on her shirt. Diego scrambled to climb closer, stretching his leg out and landing an awkward kick on Agent Brown's forehead. Agent Brown let go of Samantha and grabbed Diego's foot, trying to pull him off the metal structure to his death. Samantha screamed and climbed back toward Agent Brown.

The breeze rippled Diego's shirt as Agent Brown's hand tightened around his ankle. Diego gripped the metal bars and tried to pull himself free. Samantha moved sideways along the metal latticework. She could've got away. Why was she risking her life for him?

Samantha took one hand off the metal bars and twisted Agent Brown's ear. The agent yelled in protest and let go of Diego's foot. Samantha moved laterally across the scaffold to escape. Diego watched in horror as Agent Brown clamped a hand on top of Samantha's and pulled her hand from the bar. She swung by one hand, her feet scrambling to find a foothold. She lost her grip with the second hand and fell. Diego felt as though a linebacker had slammed into his chest as he watched her drop.

She fell several feet before landing on a section of scaffolding that extended farther out to accommodate a decorative feature. She grabbed hold of the metal latticework before she slipped off the edge. Diego climbed down to get to her. She was home free if she'd use one of the ladders and not try to rescue him again.

Sirens sounded in the distance. He could see police cars weaving through streets toward them. Someone must have seen them and called 911. Either that or the agents had alerted the locals. Agent Brown had been making his way toward Diego, but when the sirens sounded, he switched direction and climbed up a story onto the scaffold that bordered an open floor.

Diego was tired of this. Agent Brown wasn't getting away again. He climbed up and out onto the floor where Agent Brown had disappeared. When he stepped out onto the floor, it was quiet.

The sirens grew louder and closer. He saw movement behind some plastic that had been hung from the ceiling. He ran across the floor, slipping behind the plastic. It was dark in this corner of the building. He waited for his eyes to adjust.

Agent Brown pounced on him from behind. Diego spun around and hit Brown hard against the jaw. He swung back. The two men wrestled to the floor, rolling across the wooden subfloor exchanging blows until Agent Brown was on top of Diego. He grabbed Diego's collar. Then Agent Brown drew his arm back, preparing to hit him.

Outside, the sirens stopped. The police must have arrived. Brown let go of Diego, jumped to his feet and ran. Diego flipped over, stood up and chased after him.

Down below, he could hear the clamor of the police as they raced up the stairs. They wouldn't get here in time to stop Agent Brown. It was up to him. He heard footsteps pound on wood and caught a glimpse of movement. Brown had slipped down a hole that looked like an empty elevator shaft. It ran all the way to the first floor. Diego grabbed the same cable Agent Brown had used and slid down. The first floor was too dark to see much of anything.

Someone must have directed the police to the upper floors because the first floor was completely silent. Diego hit the ground and started searching.

He raced down an unfinished hallway toward a door that opened up into an outside area full of heavy equipment and building supplies. Shielding his eyes from the sun, he searched for Agent Brown. He scanned the entire area, checking everywhere he could think of before he gave up. He slammed a fist into his palm. Agent Brown had eluded him again.

# NINETEEN

Samantha raced up the stairs, frantic to know that Diego was safe.

One of the officers turned around and faced her. "You'd be best off staying downstairs by the patrol cars."

She hadn't told the police everything, only that two men were fighting and that there was a danger they might kill each other.

She pushed past him. "I have to see if he's okay."

Upstairs, she found only some blood spattered across the floor behind some plastic hanging from the ceiling.

She placed a trembling hand over her mouth. She saw the possibility of a life without Diego in it, and it made her heartsick. She cared deeply about him. She could at least admit that. "Where…do you suppose they are?"

One of the officers looked down a huge square cut in the floor. "This looks like it'll be an elevator or staircase—maybe they went down this way?"

"Samantha." A warm voice caressed her ears.

She whirled around. Diego stood before her, his face bloody. There was a look of weariness in his posture and expression, but he was alive. Her heart leaped. She ran toward him.

He wrapped his arms around her. She pressed close to him, affection bursting through her.

"I thought something had happened to you and I—" Her voice broke.

He gazed down at her, eyes filled with adoration. "No, *dulce novia*, I always make it through. Diego Cruz is a survivor."

She shook her head and touched his cheek, wiping the blood away. His expression changed. His mouth tightened. "Agent Brown got away."

"I'm sure they are looking for him," she said.

Pam and Agent Klark came up the stairs.

Pam spoke first. "Look, you two. You have been through enough today. Let's get you to that safe house. We'll take Samantha's statement there."

Agent Klark put his hands on his hips. "We don't want to risk any more interference as long as Agent Brown is at large."

"We have a car waiting," added Pam.

They walked down the stairs and out into the sunlight. The two agents sat in the front. Diego opened the back door for Samantha. She caught him glancing around before he went to his side of the car. He was probably still hoping to see Agent Brown, to get him.

He yanked open the opposite door and sat in the seat beside her.

She saw the tightness of his jaw, that look of intense focus on his face.

"They are going to catch him." She placed her hand over his, hoping to reassure him.

"*I* want to be the one who catches him," he said.

Diego was driven by a strong sense of justice. She liked that about him.

Agent Klark spoke without turning around. "The entire Everett police force is looking for him."

They drove out of town along a winding two-lane road into the forest. Gradually the Sound came back into view. They parked the car close to the pier.

So the safe house was actually a safe boat.

Pam turned to face them. "Not what you expected, right?"

"No," Samantha said.

"After we get your statement, we've got another agent coming to watch over you until Agent Brown is in custody."

"He said he had ways to get out of the country quickly. Do you suppose he'll just leave?" That was her hope. Now that the law was breathing down his neck, wouldn't he want to save himself and not risk getting caught by coming after them?

"If he is as connected, as Diego suggests, all the way up to the number two man in the Northwest, he probably does have a way to leave the country," Agent Klark said. "But if he was planning to do that, I think he already would have by now."

"As tenacious as he's been," said Pam, "I wonder if he wasn't told to take you two out before he could leave."

The thought chilled Samantha to the bone, but it explained why Agent Brown hadn't immediately used his contacts to leave the country.

The two agents led them to the boat and below deck.

"Diego, you probably want to get some sleep," said Pam. "There's a bed in the forward cabin."

Diego nodded and disappeared. Agent Klark opened his laptop and proceeded to ask Samantha questions about everything that had happened. Though they were told they were safe and her testimony was now on record if something did happen to her, Samantha could not let go of her anxiety. It seemed like years since she'd felt as if she didn't have to be looking over her shoulder and in fear for her life.

Diego awoke to the hum of a motor and the sensation that the boat was moving. Alarmed, he bolted upright in the bed and dashed to the main cabin. Samantha was sitting at the table with a sandwich and an open Bible.

She looked serene. The overhead light bathed her in a golden glow. "Is everything all right?" she asked when he came bursting in. She seemed calm enough.

"Why are we leaving the harbor?"

She brushed her hand over a page of the Bible. "The agent they sent to guard us knows how to drive a boat. He said we'd be a lot safer if we were out on open water. That way, no one can sneak up on us."

"So they didn't catch Agent Brown?"

Her features altered as though a shadow had fallen across her face. "No, they weren't able to find him in Everett."

He sat down beside her.

"Are you hungry? There's sandwich stuff," she said.

He touched his stomach. When had he last eaten? "Yeah, starving."

She rose, opened the refrigerator and pulled out cold cuts and cheese. He leaned so he could have a view of the open Bible. She was reading the Psalms.

"It came with the boat," she said. She took some bread out of a bag. "My father always said if you're trying to find a way back into the Bible, the Psalms is a good place to start."

"Are you trying to find a way back?"

"My home and community weren't the only things I lost because of Eric." She set her jaw, and for the first time since he'd known her, he detected rage in her voice. "Eric used to sit in church grinning. Ingratiating himself with everyone. Talking the Jesus talk."

Her anger revealed the depth of her pain and confusion. "That wasn't God. That was Eric." He spoke gently.

She slathered mustard on the bread and assembled the sandwich. She pulled a glass from a cupboard and poured milk in it. "It's hard to separate the two sometimes." She set the sandwich in front of him and then took a seat on the other side of the table. "Every time I walk into a church, I think of Eric."

He pushed the Bible toward her. "I can see how that would be hard. You associate everything connected to church with him."

"In my head, I know God didn't cause the pain."

He placed his palm on his chest. "But it's a different story in here, right?" He'd been where she was once. When his mother died, he knew he had a choice to make, to follow God or to be consumed by bitterness and, for him, guilt.

Her whole demeanor softened. "Yes, exactly." She held him in the magnetic pull of her gaze.

The boat creaked and groaned as waves splashed against it and the engine hummed.

"We can go topside after you eat, if you like. Agent Smith said he'd kill the engine and we could just sail. I said I would help him."

"You know how to sail, do you?"

"Yes." She cast her gaze down at the table. "I guess

there wasn't much opportunity for sailing where you grew up." She seemed embarrassed or apologetic.

"It's all right, Samantha. You and I are more alike than I could see at first." And he meant that. It made him kind of heartsick to think that when this was all over they might have to part ways. He pushed the Bible toward her again. "I hope you find your way back."

He ate his sandwich and gulped his milk while she read. This was the one thing they had not had since they'd been on the island, a quiet moment together without fear encroaching on the experience.

The sound of the motor died out and a voice shouted down at them from the deck. "Smooth sailing, if you're interested."

"You want to go topside with me? It's a beautiful night."

He nodded. He'd slept for a long time if it was night already. They climbed the ladder. A million stars filled the sky.

"Diego, this is Agent Smith." Samantha indicated the stocky man leaning against the railing.

Diego held out his hand for Agent Smith to shake. His grip was a little weak. Diego couldn't see the man's face in the darkness.

"I'll get that mainsail eased," said Samantha.

Diego stood beside Agent Smith. "Nice night, huh?" He could see the lights of other boats in the distance. One looked as if it was coming directly toward them.

"Yes," said Agent Smith. He scooted a little distance away from Diego.

The agent was giving off a strange vibe that didn't make much sense to Diego. They didn't even know each other, yet something about Agent Smith seemed almost hostile.

"So are you from the Everett field office? I don't remember seeing you there." The other boat continued to come toward them, showing no sign of veering in one direction or the other.

Agent Smith pushed away from the railing. "I'm from the Tacoma office. Low man on the totem pole gets guard duty."

Diego felt a tightening in his chest. Agents from the Tacoma office had done joint task with the Seattle field office.

Samantha continued to fuss with the sail. She stopped, straightened up and stared out at the approaching boat.

"I just want you to know I have medical bills for my kid to pay." Agent Smith took another step away from the railing.

"What?" said Diego. Even though he could not process what Agent Smith had told him, he knew they were in danger.

"Why isn't that boat turning?" Fear saturated Samantha's voice.

"The drug cartel has deep pockets and Agent Brown has extensive connections." Agent Smith took another step back.

He could hear the clacking of the other boat's engine as it drew alongside them. Agent Smith leaped into the water and swam the short distance to the other boat, which had stopped maybe ten feet from them.

Samantha backed away from the sail.

Diego couldn't see anyone moving above deck on the other boat. What exactly did they have planned?

"Start the engine," he told Samantha. She scrambled down below deck.

Agent Smith arrived at the other boat and climbed up the ladder. Still no sign of any other people.

The engine of their boat sputtered and died several times. Agent Smith had probably sabotaged it. They had to get off this boat.

He shouted down at Samantha. "Back up here. We need to get out the life raft."

He reached down for Samantha's hand and pulled her up. Now he saw someone on the deck of the other boat. The shadows were hard to discern, but it looked as if a man was kneeling, setting something up.

They scrambled to the far side of the boat. Both of them worked to untie the life raft. It splashed as it hit the water. Samantha started down the ladder toward the water.

Diego detected a pop and a hissing sound right before the boat exploded and splintered into a thousand pieces.

The impact of the bomb jerked Samantha off the ladder. She plunged into the water, losing all sense of direction. She righted herself and swam up toward the surface. As she broke through the water, debris rained down on her. She was at least forty feet from the boat, which swayed to one side. An entire side of the boat was missing. The ocean consumed it by degrees. She treaded water, turning slightly. She couldn't see Diego or the life raft. The other boat moved forward in the water and then started to turn.

They were searching to make sure she and Diego hadn't survived. Even though she was already shivering, she plunged back beneath the surface of the water.

A piece of wood floated by. She grabbed hold of it, keeping her head just above the surface so she could see and breathe—while hopefully remaining unseen.

A man on the deck of the boat angled a searchlight across the water. When the light illuminated the area around her, she slipped back beneath the water. The boat got so close to her its wake pushed her back in the water. She waited for the light to disappear before resurfacing.

When she came up, the boat was about ten feet from her. She could see Diego clinging to the back of it, holding on to the ropes and resting his feet on a narrow runner.

He saw her and waved her over. She swam toward him. The motor revved as the boat prepared to take off. She stroked through the water faster. Diego reached out for her and pulled her up.

She shivered. "Is this a good idea?"

As the boat gained speed, she could hear men talking. When she looked up, she had a view of a pair of legs.

Diego leaned close. "Agent Brown is on this boat. I'm not letting him get away again."

While she agreed that Agent Brown needed to be stopped, she'd seen what he was capable of. If they tried to capture him, they might both end up dead.

Feet pounded across the deck. The voices faded. Diego lifted his head to view the deck. "We're clear. Hide behind that storage bin." He gestured that she should go up first.

Her arms stretched as she strained to pull herself on deck. Diego pushed her up from below. She crawled to the rectangular storage bin. Diego was right behind her. She peered into the bow of the boat, where the men had gone. Two men, Agent Brown and another man, stood in the warm glow of the bridge talking. There may have been a third man in the shadows.

Diego eased the storage bin open and felt around. He pulled out a blanket and a towel. He offered her the blanket, which she wrapped around her shoulders.

"I don't see Agent Smith."

Diego leaned close to her ear and whispered, "Once the explosion cleared, he got back in the water. The Coast Guard was probably alerted about the explosion by other boats who saw it. I suspect that the plan was that Agent Smith will tell them he was thrown clear by the explosion but that we're dead. Coast Guard will assume it was drug related."

She could pick up snippets of the conversation. It sounded as if Agent Brown's plan was to head to Canada. From there, he would probably escape to somewhere he could never be found.

A sense of righteous indignation rose up in her. It wasn't right that he get off scot-free. She wanted justice as badly as Diego did.

"What do we do?"

"I see three guys. They probably all have guns. We need to take one of them out without alerting the other two and get a gun."

"So we wait until one of them comes back up on deck alone."

Diego nodded. "I'm going to move in a little closer and hide." He cupped his hand on her shoulder. "Be ready."

Diego crawled along the deck, hiding in the shadows that the high sides of the boat provided. She felt his absence immediately. Having him close always made her feel safer.

The darkness seemed to intensify as the boat sped

through the water. One of the men said something about getting some sleep and disappeared. The hours crept by. Her legs cramped, and she repositioned herself.

Diego moved in and out of the shadows. Maybe he was growing impatient, too. She knew they had to wait for the exact right moment or they would both get killed. The only thing they had on their side was the element of surprise. Agent Brown thought they were dead.

The blanket helped cut out some of the evening's chill, but not all. She stared up at the night sky, stars twinkling above her. The conversation between the two men died out. She lifted her head and looked over the storage bin. The men were both still on the bridge by the wheel but no longer talking.

Waves slapped the side of the boat. They passed another boat headed the other way. Loud party noises and bright lights emanated from the other craft. When the noise was at its zenith, the man who wasn't Agent Brown turned and moved out onto the deck.

He stepped out only a few feet, probably to see what the party boat was doing. The joyful noises died away and the bright lights got smaller. She turned her attention back to the boat she was on.

The stranger had stepped out on deck, but not too far from the bridge. If they tackled him now, Agent Brown would be alerted. The stranger took a few more steps in their direction. Just a little farther and they could hope to overtake him without getting caught.

Her breathing sounded incredibly loud. Her heart pounded. She had no way to communicate with Diego. She just had to trust that they would both choose the same moment. They had only one chance.

The stranger wandered over to the opposite side of

the boat from where Diego was. He leaned against the railing and stared out at the water.

*Now*, she thought. *It has to be now.*

# TWENTY

From the shadows where he crouched, Diego watched. He could see the hired thug in silhouette as he leaned against the railing. He waited for the exact right moment when the thug's guard was down. The man's shoulders relaxed.

Diego pounced like a lion, landing on the man's back and taking him to the ground. He hoped the thud of a body falling wouldn't bring trouble. He pinned the man down face-first and cupped a hand over his mouth.

"Not a word." Diego spoke through gritted teeth.

Samantha was at his side. She'd been so quick and silent. He hadn't even noticed her coming.

"I've got his gun," she said.

"Get something to tie him up and gag him with." He glanced toward the bow of the boat. Agent Brown still stood at the wheel with his back to them. The scuffle hadn't caught his attention.

Samantha searched the area around her, crouching and watching the front of the boat, as well.

Diego's captive resisted only a little. That was the problem with hired muscle. Their heart wasn't in the fight. Anyone connected to the drug trade Diego sought to destroy would be more dangerous.

Samantha crawled toward Diego. "Some wire is all I could find and this." She held up a scrap of fabric.

"Good. Get that in his mouth." He took the wire and wrapped it around the man's wrists while she gagged him with the fabric.

"What are you doing?" A voice boomed above them.

It was the third man. He must have been awakened when the man's body fell on the deck. Diego saw now that the third man was Scarface from the zoo. He stomped toward him. Diego glanced around. Samantha must have hidden. Smart woman. The gun was still on the deck about three feet from Diego. He lunged toward it.

Scarface stomped on Diego's hand with his boot and kicked the gun across the deck. Intense pain shot up Diego's arm, distracting him as Scarface reached down and picked Diego up by the shoulders. Diego managed to kick the other man's ankles before he was lifted up and tossed. His back slammed against the railing.

Scarface fought like a man who had something to lose.

Diego dived toward the man who was substantially bigger than he, slamming against him with all his weight. Colliding with him was like running into a brick wall. He punched him in the stomach twice and once across the jaw. Scarface recovered quickly and raised a fist to hit Diego. Diego feared the noise of the scuffle would alert Agent Brown.

The boat rocked more intensely, swaying from side to side. They'd hit some choppy water, which must be occupying Brown's focus.

Diego's feet were pulled out from beneath him, and both men slid to one side of the boat and then back to the other side.

Scarface grabbed Diego's leg and pulled him close.

Diego swung at the other man, but only managed to take a swipe at air as the boat rocked and the men slid along the deck. Water spread over the top of the deck.

Diego wondered where Samantha had hidden. In seas this rough, they should be below deck. He tried to grab hold of something stable. The waves continued to rock the boat. Salt water sprayed his face.

Scarface had given up the fight as well, in favor of staying alive. The bound man slipped toward the back of the boat. He lay on his side, struggling to get into a sitting position.

Diego glanced toward the front of the boat, where Agent Brown was frantically trying to steer the boat through the rough seas. Now would be the perfect time to ambush him.

Diego crawled soldier style toward the bow, not daring to stand up for fear of being washed overboard. Scarface came after him, moving in the same manner. He worried that Samantha had already been dragged into the rough water. He cleared his mind of the images that the thought created. He needed to keep his focus on the fight at hand. If he searched for her, he'd only expose her presence to Scarface—and possibly Brown, as well. She'd proved over and over she could take care of herself. He said a quick prayer for her safety.

Scarface grabbed his ankle. Another wave washed over the deck. Diego tried to twist free of Scarface's grasp. The larger man dragged Diego toward him and punched him in the face.

Samantha appeared out of the shadows and hit Scarface on the side of the head with some kind of object. The man collapsed on the deck unconscious.

"Perfect timing," Diego shouted above the roar of the storm.

"We need to get below deck," she said. "Help me with these guys or they'll drown."

She was right. They couldn't leave them on deck to die. Whatever they had done, they were human beings. They helped the smaller man get below deck, and together they moved an unconscious Scarface and tied him up. They shut the two men in the bathroom.

Diego slid down to the floor as exhaustion invaded his body. Bombarded by the waves, the boat continued to sway and jerk. "We have to stop Agent Brown before he gets to Canada."

She opened a cupboard, pulled out a towel and tossed it to him. "Now would be the time. He's distracted with trying to navigate through the storm."

Diego did his best to dry off with the towel. A chill sank into his bones that probably wouldn't leave for weeks. "We'll have to go back up on deck to get to him."

She nodded. Both of them knew what a risk they were taking going back out and attempting to take down the man who was guiding their boat through the storm. "At least it will be two against one."

But the one they were up against had a gun and murder in his heart. "I'll go first. Once we get across the deck, I'll wait for a moment when he's distracted to jump in and take him down," said Diego.

There were a thousand things that could go wrong. The boat could be hit by a wave big enough to send them into the ocean. Agent Brown could hear them coming and shoot them both. But this was their last, best chance.

Samantha tilted her head as the boat listed to one side. "We'd better do this."

He detected the fear beneath her words, but appreciated her attempt to sound brave. They made their way up the ladder as the boat rocked. A blast of sideways rain hit his face when he poked his head up out of the cabin. He pulled himself on deck and crawled forward. Samantha's head appeared. He reached out his arm for her to hold on to as she hoisted herself on deck.

She looked up, her expression growing grim.

Diego turned his head slowly. Agent Brown stood behind them with a gun in his hand.

The fabric on Diego's shirt brushed against her cheek as he scooted between Samantha and Agent Brown. They were both on their knees. The boat listed substantially to one side, making them slide across the deck. She heard a shot being fired and pinging off something metal.

Agent Brown couldn't stay away from the helm for long, not in water this rough. When she looked up, he had gone back to steer the boat.

The boat was almost on its side. Diego's strong arms wrapped around her waist. If they stayed out here much longer, the ocean would do Agent Brown's job for him. They'd be washed out to sea and drowned.

Agent Brown stepped out again to fire off another shot and then returned to manning the boat. Gripping the metal railing, Diego worked his way toward the front of the boat.

She shouted above the roar of the waves. "He'll shoot us when we get there."

Agent Brown had shut and probably locked the doors to the bridge to keep water from flowing in.

"He's focused on preventing this boat from capsizing," he said. "We have to try."

Another wave washed over the boat. Diego nearly lost

his grip on her. She struggled to grasp the railing like he was doing. He worked his way toward the doors.

The boat righted itself somewhat but still leaned to one side.

She huddled behind him, leaning close to shout into his ear. "Wait until the next big wave comes. He'll be distracted. Maybe we can kick the door open."

Diego nodded. "Good plan."

She stared out into the dark ocean and watched the huge wave looming toward the boat, a wall of water that could send them into the depths.

They'd have to let go of the railing to get close enough to the door. The wave drew closer. This was a plan that could cost both of them their lives.

Resolve like liquid steel coursed through her. She was not going to let Agent Brown win. Not after fighting this hard.

Diego gazed out into the ocean. "Now," he said.

They scooted forward and both banged on the wooden door with their feet. The door flung open. The wave rushed over the deck. They threw themselves into the engine room as salt water filled it.

Agent Brown reached for his gun.

Again the boat tipped, the wooden hull creaking from the force of the water.

Diego managed to get to his feet. He jumped Agent Brown, slamming his body against the other man's. The gunshot was insanely loud in the enclosed room.

Her breath caught, and fear coursed through her as she waited for Diego's limp body to fall to the wet floor.

Instead, he punched Agent Brown hard in the stomach, making the man double over. Then she saw the gun sliding across the floor as water flowed in.

The boat rocked wildly. Agent Brown slammed into Diego, pushing him to the ground. Samantha was propelled against a back wall, the wind momentarily knocked out of her.

Diego and Agent Brown wrestled on the floor. She looked at the waves coming toward them. Someone needed to be steering this boat or they would all die. She stepped behind the helm and assessed the best way to get around the approaching waves.

Agent Brown managed to get on top of Diego. He pushed Diego's face into the rising water, trying to drown him. She let go of the wheel and searched for the gun, picked it up and hit Agent Brown in the head with it.

The blow was enough to get the agent off Diego but not enough to knock him out. Diego twisted up onto his knees.

"I have the gun." Her hands were shaking.

Agent Brown sneered. "You don't know how to use that."

Agent Brown was between her and Diego.

"Just pull the trigger, right?" Her bluff fooled no one.

Diego had managed to rise to his feet.

The boat rocked to and fro, banging her against the wall. She dropped the gun. Both Diego and Agent Brown dived for it. She caught sight of the next wave coming toward them and turned her attention back to steering the boat.

Neither man got to the gun before the rising water swallowed it. Agent Brown lifted Diego up and slammed him against the wall, then punched him.

She could see calmer waters up ahead. She steered toward them.

Diego slipped down to the floor, clutching his stomach. Agent Brown pounced on him. She left the wheel to try to help Diego. She beat on Agent Brown's back. "Get off him."

The distraction bought Diego enough time to stand. He punched Agent Brown hard across the jaw.

The two men continued to fight. Samantha picked up the radio and put out a distress call to the Coast Guard, alerting them of their location and situation. The sea continued to be rough but no longer life threatening.

Diego knocked Agent Brown to the floor. "Got something to tie him up with?"

Agent Brown continued to resist, attempting to twist free. Diego placed a knee in the middle of his back and held his hands behind him.

Samantha searched the room, coming up with some rope. She handed it to Diego.

The Coast Guard sirens sounded in the distance. Diego pulled the bound Agent Brown to his feet and propped him against the wall. He stepped back out on deck and returned with more rope to tie the agent's feet.

Diego wiped the blood from his face. "You didn't think you were going to get away, did you?"

Agent Brown sneered and shook his head. "Can't blame a guy for trying."

The Coast Guard boat appeared on the horizon. Though she felt as if she might collapse, Samantha took in a breath.

A few minutes later, the Coast Guard boat came alongside their vessel. Diego moved toward the door. "I've got to explain the situation to them." He placed his palm on her cheek. "You'll be all right?" He tilted his head toward Agent Brown.

She stared up into Diego's wide, dark eyes. "He's not going anywhere."

Diego left the bridge.

She looked directly at Agent Brown. "And I'm not afraid of him anymore."

Agent Brown lifted an eyebrow. "I'd fear for my life if I was in your shoes, honey. You have no idea what's in store for you."

His words chilled her. What did he mean by that? She squared her shoulders and looked him in the eye. "You're going to jail for a long time."

He laughed. "You won't be safe…ever."

The sound of his laughter still echoed in her ears when Diego returned. "They'll take him and the other two into custody."

He held a hand out for her. "Let's get you someplace warm and dry."

She was shaking from the physical exertion and the emotional trauma. He wrapped his arm around her, steadied her until a female Coast Guard member met her at the boat railing.

The Coast Guard woman studied them. "Looks like you've had a bad day at the office."

Samantha gazed at Diego. She'd lived a lifetime in the few short days she'd been with him. Everything after this would seem mundane.

His face glowed with affection. He brushed his fingers up and down her arm. What was he thinking? He clearly cared for her, but their worlds had intersected by chance. What would happen to them now that they had no reason to stay together any longer?

"I'm Chief Petty Officer Neill," said the Coast Guard woman. "Come this way. I'll show you where you can get cleaned up and find you some dry clothes."

Samantha followed Officer Neill's lead to a bathroom

with a shower. "They'll be some dry clothes waiting for you when you get out." The female officer excused herself, shutting the door on the way out.

Samantha stepped into the shower. The hot water soothed her, but she could not let go of what Agent Brown had said to her about fearing for her life, the way he'd laughed as if he had one more trick up his sleeve.

When she emerged from the shower, a sweatshirt that said Coast Guard and sweatpants were laid out on a chair. She got dressed and gingerly opened the door.

Diego sat in one of the cabin chairs. Agent Brown and his two thugs must be in a separate area of the boat. At least she wouldn't have to listen to his threats anymore.

Diego had changed into dry clothes, as well. He wore the same sweat outfit she'd been given.

"Twins." He offered her his charming smile, the one she'd been so suspicious of when she'd first met him. She knew better now. He was nothing like Eric.

She took a seat opposite him, still feeling shaken and uneasy. "Agent Brown is restrained?"

Diego pointed. "They have a sort of holding cell in the forward cabin."

She took in a breath, trying to relax.

"I've been on the phone with Gabriel. He says it looks like Agent Brown would alert the drug network of what the Bureau's next move was in exchange for a bigger and bigger piece of the drug trade. We suspect an IT guy was involved, too, and that's how Agent Brown got a lot of his information."

"Sounds like there is a decent case against him," she said.

"Yeah, but I'm pretty sure my job is over. I can't hope to work undercover as a CI, not in this city, anyway."

So Diego was thinking about leaving Seattle. "I'm

sure you'll figure out how to make a difference. That's what your work was about anyway."

He studied her for a long moment. "Yes, it is."

"I haven't known you that long, Diego, but you seemed the happiest when you were playing basketball with those boys outside your sister's house."

Diego nodded as though he were thinking about what she said. "I suppose."

So much was going unsaid between them. She wished she could tell him how she felt. That she cared deeply for him, but what could they do about it? She glanced around the room. The couch on the opposite side of the room looked very inviting. "I think I might get some sleep."

He shifted his weight in the chair. "You should do that." He studied her for a long moment.

She pulled free of the magnetic power of his gaze and curled up on the couch facing away from him. Her eyelids felt heavy as the fog of sleep rolled in.

Just as she was drifting off, Diego put a blanket over her. Her eyes warmed with tears. She was going to miss that tenderness. A few minutes later, she heard him get up and leave the cabin.

After covering Samantha with a blanket, Diego went on deck, stared out at the ocean and breathed in the salt air. He was exhausted beyond belief, but staying in the same room with Samantha had been too hard. Once they got back to shore, they would have no reason to stay together.

He had come to really care about her, but he could offer her nothing. He had no job. He was going to have to rebuild his life from the ground up. As far as he knew, there could be some sort of bounty on his head. He might have to leave the state.

He'd never liked goodbyes, and this one was really going to hurt. The thought of looking into those blue eyes again tore him up. Maybe it would be better if they didn't have a formal parting.

He watched as the shore drew closer. When the boat docked, he disembarked and walked out into the Seattle night.

# TWENTY-ONE

Samantha wiped the sweat from her brow and stared at the gleaming kitchen she'd just cleaned. She was on another island preparing for another party. This one was being thrown by a father who wanted to celebrate his daughter turning sixteen.

She'd gone back to her job at Evergreen Catering because she liked it. This was her life now. Even if Eric did eventually leave Cambridge Heights, she knew she couldn't return there. She was not the same person, and she didn't want what Cambridge Heights offered.

She gathered up her cleaning supplies and stepped out into the sunlight. There were residents on this island a few miles away, and the event facilities were certainly more pristine than they had been at the island where she'd met Diego.

It had been a month since she'd awakened as the Coast Guard boat pulled into the harbor. By the time she'd got on deck, Diego had already disembarked. Maybe it was better that way. No awkward goodbye, or worse, a weak promise to get together for coffee sometime in the future. How could they do something as ordinary as have coffee together after all they had been through?

She missed him. The memory of the one kiss they'd shared was seared into her brain. She walked across the grounds to the car she'd brought with her on the ferry. She put the cleaning supplies away and walked up to a cliff that looked out on the ocean. She sat down on a bench, closed her eyes and thanked God for the beautiful day. It was good to be talking to Him again.

"I've been watching you. Waiting for a chance to find you alone."

Her blood froze in her veins. "Eric." She didn't turn around. Seeing his face would only drive the terror deeper into her psyche. "How did you find me?"

"An FBI agent called me, trying to figure out who you were. He was doing some kind of background check on you. I told him how bad I wanted to find you. I was able to get the information from him that you worked at a catering company. Took me a while to figure out which one. Apparently, you took up with some drug dealer."

Anger surged through her at the misrepresentation of Diego's character. She purged her voice of all emotion. So that was what Agent Brown's threat meant. He must have picked up on Eric's vendetta for her and given Eric enough information to find her. "There are people here on this island."

He leaned over her and spoke in her ear. "They're quite far away, my dear." His hand wrapped around the back of her neck. "Nobody leaves Eric James. I told you that. Do you know what you did to my reputation?"

She knew the smartest thing to do would be to appear to cooperate and wait for the chance to get away. "I'm so sorry, Eric. Clearly, I've hurt you deeply. I'll come with you."

She stood up with his hand still clamped around her

neck. He came around to her side of the bench and shoved her toward the edge of the cliff.

"It would be so easy to kill you." He ran a finger over the scars on her neck and chest. The touch was his way of reminding her what he was capable of. His hot breath pummeled her ear.

She swallowed her fear. "Eric, I said I would go with you."

He spoke through gritted teeth. "Yes, you will." He shoved her hard.

Her feet reached the edge of the cliff, pushing loose rocks that tumbled down the steep incline. She wobbled. Down below, two people walking on the beach stopped and stared up at her, shading their eyes from the sun. He yanked her back by the collar of her shirt and then gave the walkers a friendly wave as if to say *everything's okay up here*.

"It would be that easy, sweetheart." He spit out his words as though they were rocks in his mouth. He wrapped his hand around her hair, drawing it up into a ponytail.

Had he meant to kill her or just scare her? She wasn't sure. When they were married, he had kept her in line with words and the threat of physical violence. But today, he seemed angrier and more out of control than she'd ever seen him. "What are you going to do, Eric?"

"Don't ask any more questions. Just walk down this hill."

She trudged forward. She couldn't hope to get away as long as he held on to her hair. Or could she? She was a different person from the frightened child who had run from him over a year ago. Her time with Diego had taught her that she was stronger than she realized. She could fight her way free if she had to. She didn't have to be stronger than Eric; she just had to be more clever.

She quickened her pace down the hill.

"Slow down," Eric said.

She stopped abruptly. In the moment that Eric was caught off guard, she twisted around and punched him in the stomach. He let go of her hair. She darted away and raced toward her car. She'd left the keys in the cup holder. If she could reach the car, she'd have a fighting chance for escape.

His feet pounded behind her. She ran faster, her leg muscles on fire from the exertion. The car was twenty feet away. She reached out for the door handle. His fingers grazed her neck. She whirled around and kicked him in the shin and then pushed him before he could recover from the first blow.

The look of shock on his face as he tumbled to the ground was worth a million dollars.

*That's right, Eric. I'm not the same shrinking violet you nearly destroyed.*

She yanked open the door. Eric crawled across the ground and grabbed her ankle, pulling her through the dirt. Terror seized her heart. Now she saw the rage in his eyes. She tried to twist away, but he put all his weight on her chest. He lunged at her neck, clamping on and squeezing.

She clawed and scraped his hands as black dots appeared around the edges of her vision. She fought for air.

"No one crosses Eric James." His teeth showed, and he squeezed tighter.

She wasn't going to let him win. She would fight him to the very end. Even as she struggled for breath, she lifted her leg in an effort to knee him in the back. The action only made him angrier. Her vision had gone almost completely dark.

Then suddenly the pressure on her neck evaporated. She took in her first rattling breath and blinked in an effort to focus. The thumping and grunting of two men in a fight reached her ears. Her vision cleared.

Diego had pinned Eric to the ground.

A hundred questions raged through her as she pushed herself to her feet. What was he doing here? How did he know she needed him? Diego managed to subdue Eric.

"Let me guess—you want something to tie him up with?" she said.

Diego's chest heaved from the effort of the fight, but he managed a nod. "We seem to be making this a habit."

She rifled around in her car until she came up with a bungee cord.

"You won't get away with this." Eric lifted his head, spitting out his words. "Assaulting me. Tying me up."

Samantha rolled her eyes and shook her head. How convenient that he forgot that he nearly choked her. That was typical for the sociopath. Nothing was ever his fault. Eric was always the wronged one.

Diego stood on his feet. "Actually, you're the one who is going to have assault charges filed against you, my friend. I saw what you did to her."

Diego stepped away from Eric, who let a string of curses fly from his mouth. He led Samantha away and pulled out his phone. "I think there is a deputy or some sort of law enforcement on the island."

He called for help. They waited until the deputy showed up and hauled Eric away.

She stepped toward Diego. "What made you come out here today?"

"I got a call from a man earlier today asking questions about you and me, like how we were connected. He didn't identify himself, but I had a feeling it was Eric," Diego said. "I remembered where you worked. When they said another man had been by earlier today asking about you, alarm bells went off."

"And so you found me."

He reached out and touched her cheek with the back of his hand. "I think I would have come for you sooner or later even if it wasn't an emergency."

She tilted her head to one side as her heart fluttered. "What do you mean?"

"All this time, I thought I either had to fit into your world or you had to fit into mine. Then I realized, why can't we make a whole new world together in another city helping gang kids?" His stare was pensive as he waited for her answer.

Was he asking to marry her? She wasn't sure.

"You said the time I seemed the happiest was when I was playing B-ball with those boys. I don't know why we can't just work this problem from the other end. Keep them from ever breaking the law."

"Yes, of course. I can see how that would work." She was still trying to understand what he was saying. "And you want me to be your...partner?"

Diego slammed the heel of his hand into his forehead and said something in Spanish. He grabbed both of her hands and looked into her eyes. "No, I'm an idiot who's explaining this very badly. What I want is for you to be my wife."

She felt suddenly breathless. Wasn't this what she had wanted, too? She nodded.

He gathered her into his arms, kissing her hair and

then her lips. She rested her head against his chest as the strong arms of the man she wanted to spend her life with surrounded her.

\* \* \* \* \*

Dear Reader,

I hope you enjoyed the dangerous journey Samantha and Diego endured and the love they found together. *Mistaken Target* is about making choices in the face of tragedy. Both Samantha and Diego have lost a mom, and Samantha is still dealing with the pain of her marriage falling apart. Diego's mother died years ago, and he knew he could have been consumed by bitterness and continued the gang lifestyle, but instead he chose to follow God and to try to make Seattle a safer place. Now it is Samantha's turn to make that journey with Diego's help.

This book is personal for me because I had to make a similar choice when my husband died almost two years ago. I had to decide whether to give in to bitterness and self-pity or to stumble back to the light and love God offers. I am here to tell you that it is a moment-to-moment battle. Each day, I tell myself to get out of bed, to apologize when I'm wrong, to celebrate all that God has given me and to rebuild a life without Michael one tiny piece at a time.

Whatever loss or broken dreams you face in your own life, I pray that you are patient and forgiving toward yourself. It takes time and deliberate choosing to get back to a place of trusting God and believing that He has good things for you. Be kind to yourself, my friend.

Sharon Dunn

# REQUEST YOUR FREE BOOKS!

## 2 FREE RIVETING INSPIRATIONAL NOVELS
## PLUS 2 FREE MYSTERY GIFTS

*Love Inspired*®
# SUSPENSE
### RIVETING INSPIRATIONAL ROMANCE

**YES!** Please send me 2 FREE Love Inspired® Suspense novels and my 2 FREE mystery gifts (gifts are worth about $10). After receiving them, if I don't wish to receive any more books, I can return the shipping statement marked "cancel." If I don't cancel, I will receive 4 brand-new novels every month and be billed just $4.99 per book in the U.S. or $5.49 per book in Canada. That's a savings of at least 17% off the cover price. It's quite a bargain! Shipping and handling is just 50¢ per book in the U.S. and 75¢ per book in Canada.* I understand that accepting the 2 free books and gifts places me under no obligation to buy anything. I can always return a shipment and cancel at any time. Even if I never buy another book, the two free books and gifts are mine to keep forever.

123/323 IDN GH5Z

Name _____ (PLEASE PRINT) _____

Address _____ Apt. #

City _____ State/Prov. _____ Zip/Postal Code

Signature (if under 18, a parent or guardian must sign)

Mail to the **Reader Service:**
**IN U.S.A.:** P.O. Box 1867, Buffalo, NY 14240-1867
**IN CANADA:** P.O. Box 609, Fort Erie, Ontario L2A 5X3

**Are you a current subscriber to Love Inspired® Suspense books
and want to receive the larger-print edition?
Call 1-800-873-8635 or visit www.ReaderService.com.**

* Terms and prices subject to change without notice. Prices do not include applicable taxes. Sales tax applicable in N.Y. Canadian residents will be charged applicable taxes. Offer not valid in Quebec. This offer is limited to one order per household. Not valid for current subscribers to Love Inspired Suspense books. All orders subject to credit approval. Credit or debit balances in a customer's account(s) may be offset by any other outstanding balance owed by or to the customer. Please allow 4 to 6 weeks for delivery. Offer available while quantities last.

**Your Privacy**—The Reader Service is committed to protecting your privacy. Our Privacy Policy is available online at www.ReaderService.com or upon request from the Reader Service.
We make a portion of our mailing list available to reputable third parties that offer products we believe may interest you. If you prefer that we not exchange your name with third parties, or if you wish to clarify or modify your communication preferences, please visit us at www.ReaderService.com/consumerschoice or write to us at Reader Service Preference Service, P.O. Box 9062, Buffalo, NY 14240-9062. Include your complete name and address.

*Love Inspired*

# Love the Love Inspired book you just read?

Your opinion matters.

Review this book on your favorite book site, review site, blog or your own social media properties and share your opinion with other readers!

Be sure to connect with us at:
Harlequin.com/Newsletters
Twitter.com/LoveInspiredBks
Facebook.com/LoveInspiredBooks

HLIREVIEWSR